The Seven Wise Princesses

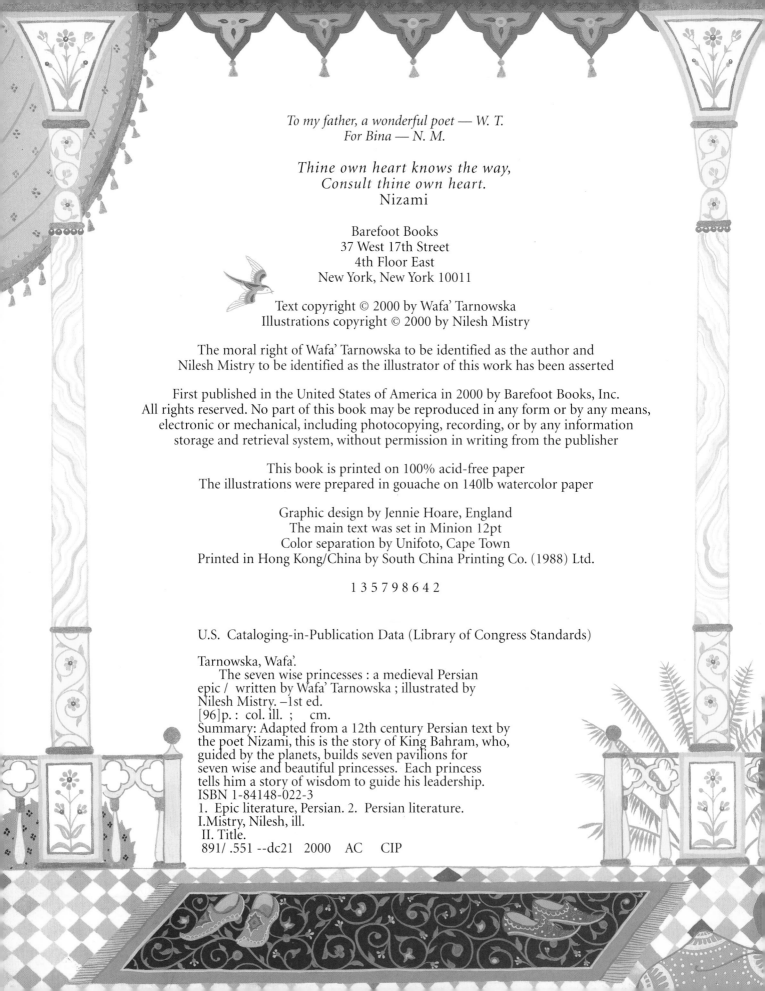

To my father, a wonderful poet — W. T.
For Bina — N. M.

Thine own heart knows the way,
Consult thine own heart.
Nizami

Barefoot Books
37 West 17th Street
4th Floor East
New York, New York 10011

Text copyright © 2000 by Wafa' Tarnowska
Illustrations copyright © 2000 by Nilesh Mistry

This book is printed on 100% acid-free paper
The illustrations were prepared in gouache on 140lb watercolor paper

Graphic design by Jennie Hoare, England
The main text was set in Minion 12pt
Color separation by Unifoto, Cape Town
Printed in Hong Kong/China by South China Printing Co. (1988) Ltd.

1 3 5 7 9 8 6 4 2

U.S. Cataloging-in-Publication Data (Library of Congress Standards)

Tarnowska, Wafa'.
    The seven wise princesses : a medieval Persian
epic / written by Wafa' Tarnowska ; illustrated by
Nilesh Mistry. –1st ed.
[96]p. : col. ill. ;   cm.
Summary: Adapted from a 12th century Persian text by
the poet Nizami, this is the story of King Bahram, who,
guided by the planets, builds seven pavilions for
seven wise and beautiful princesses. Each princess
tells him a story of wisdom to guide his leadership.
ISBN 1-84148-022-3
1. Epic literature, Persian. 2. Persian literature.
I.Mistry, Nilesh, ill.
 II. Title.
 891/ .551 --dc21 2000   AC   CIP

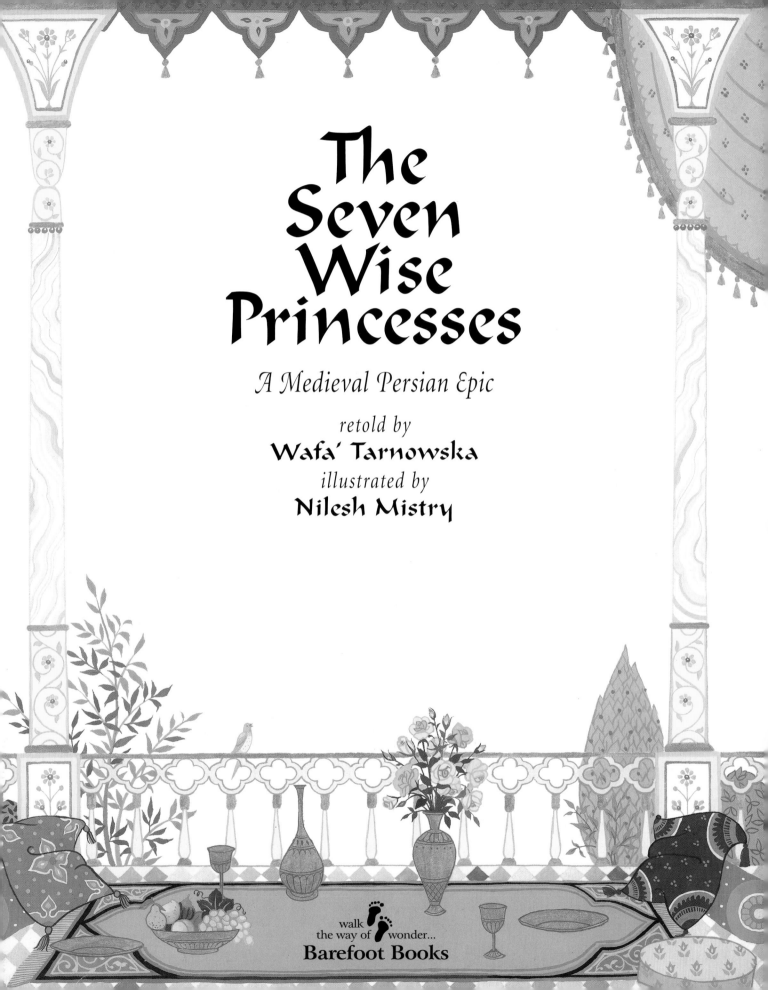

The Seven Wise Princesses

A Medieval Persian Epic

retold by
Wafa' Tarnowska
illustrated by
Nilesh Mistry

walk
the way of wonder...
Barefoot Books

Contents

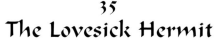

Contents

Introduction

*T*he *Seven Wise Princesses* is based on the Persian poem *Haft Paykar*, written by the medieval poet Nizami, one of the most famous Persian poets of his time, renowned for the refinement and beauty of his imagery. It is part of a series of five poems known as the *Khamsa*, or "Quintet," written in rhyming couplets.

Nizami was born in 1141 in the town of Ganja, now part of Azerbaijan. In those days, Ganja was an important and well-fortified border town, and a flourishing center of silk manufacture and trade. From 1150 onward, Ganja also became a center for poetry and literature, with Nizami a towering figure among its seven major poets.

Poetry was encouraged by the vigorous competition that existed among the various Seljuk rulers who governed the region. Although not a court poet, Nizami had some important princes for patrons. He was able to secure their support without leaving his native town, calling himself "the prisoner of Ganja." He led a very modest and quiet life, devoting himself entirely to poetry and to a Sufi group known as the Akhis, who drew their members mostly from the artisan classes. *Haft Paykar* reflects this group's ideals of human perfectibility and respect for manual labor.

Nizami's poems show that he was acquainted with Arabic and Persian literature, mathematics, geometry, astronomy, astrology, alchemy, medicine, Islamic theology, history, music, art and Sufi philosophical thought. He was a deeply religious yet not fanatical Muslim, a gentle and unostentatious loving father and husband, "combining lofty genius and blameless character in a degree unequaled by any other Persian poet," according to E. G. Browne in his *Literary History of Persia*.

Haft Paykar is considered Nizami's masterpiece. It was completed in 1197 and is an allegory for spiritual and moral growth based on the real life and exploits of the Sassanian ruler Shah Bahram V. Self-knowledge, leading to knowledge of the world and its Creator, is the principal theme of the poem. It is based on the Sufi belief that the purpose of life is to perfect oneself in preparation for the return to the Creator. The poem is also inspired by a saying of the Prophet Muhammad: "He who knows himself knows his Lord."

The second message of the *Haft Paykar* is that personal virtue and wisdom are necessary prerequisites for just rule. Shah Bahram progresses from darkness to light and from ignorance to wisdom. His visits to the seven princesses, living in seven pavilions ruled by the seven planets, parallel the Prophet's ascent to heaven as recorded in the Koran, when he passes by Saturn, the Sun, the Moon, Mars, Mercury, Jupiter and Venus. Shah Bahram's journey through the Seven Pavilions also follows the temporal order of the days of the week.

Astrology plays an important part in the poem, for Nizami, who was acquainted with astrology himself, believed that although the stars do not determine human fate, they can provide people with guidance in life.

Love is another main theme of the poem, helping Shah Bahram in his spiritual progress. The seven stories told by the princesses are about lovers and unrequited love, celebrating love as a serious pastime and mirroring the tension that exists in human hearts between desire and virtue. For in mysticism, the sublimation of sensual love is one of the paths to God.

Finally, the idea of women teaching men wisdom through storytelling is not new. It is, after all, the basis of *The Thousand and One Nights*. But what is new in Nizami's poetry is his complex image of women as strong, virtuous and sharp on the one hand and tender, passionate and beautiful on the other. It was particularly in his treatment of women that Nizami broke with the literary custom of his times.

At the age of fifty-eight, toward the end of his life, Nizami wrote the last of the *Khamsa* poems. He died sometime between 1202 and 1209 — records vary as to exactly when. The greatest Persian poets who lived after him praised him as the creator of the Persian love story, referring to him as the "Hakim" or "sage." Eight hundred years after his death, his tomb in Ganja is still a pilgrimage site.

Wafa' Tarnowska

The Making of a Shah

Once upon a time, when people asked the stars for advice on how to live, a shah called Yazdigird ruled over the land of Persia. He was fair and just, rich and kind. For him, singers composed their loveliest songs and poets their finest verses. For him, builders designed magnificent palaces and merchants traveled to faraway lands to buy the rarest spices.

Yazdigird had what all shahs should have: a strong army, a treasury filled with gold, busy markets and plentiful harvests. He had all but one thing: no son to inherit his wealth.

Years passed and Yazdigird prayed day and night for Allah to send him an heir. At last, Allah in his mercy gave him a son whom he called Bahram.

The whole empire rejoiced with their shah. Celebrations were held for forty days and forty nights. There were fireworks, banquets, concerts and dances. Royal astrologers rushed to draw the baby's horoscope, tracing the course of every planet from Jupiter to Venus, Mercury and Mars, as well as the Sun and Moon. The chief astrologer finally announced the result in front of the whole court.

"Your Majesty, your son will have a fortunate life and his name will be remembered by everyone. He will become a great shah, but, in order for this to happen, you will have to send him away to live his young days at the court of King Nu'man of Yemen. There he will grow up skilled in mathematics, astronomy, hunting and riding. He will learn to love poetry and music and to speak many languages. He will return to Persia to claim the throne after he proves himself to be worthy."

Shah Yazdigird could not argue with the chief astrologer, for astrologers in those days were as powerful as shahs. So it was with a heavy heart that he sent his one and only son to be taught and to grow up far from his homeland at the Yemeni court.

Bahram excelled at everything he did. He learned Greek, Persian and Arabic, algebra and music, but his real passion was hunting. He was so skillful that he became a legend throughout Arabia and was named Bahram Gur, which means Bahram the Hunter of Wild Donkeys.

When Bahram grew to be a young man, King Nu'man, who loved him like a son, had a special palace built for him by Simnar, one of the finest architects in the world. The palace was red and gold with a big, round dome. Its roof was like a mirror. When the rays of the sun touched it, it sparkled like a jewel. In the morning, under the deep blue of the sky, it shimmered like the sea. At night, it glittered like a giant star fallen from the sky. Bahram named his new palace Khavarnaq and lived there very comfortably.

While out hunting one day, Bahram found himself at a remote cave where no human feet had ever trod. At the entrance to the cave, a huge dragon was opening its mouth wide, ready to swallow a wild donkey. Bahram drew two arrows with his bow and aimed them at the dragon's eyes. He struck both eyes at the same time, blinding the monster with one shot. Then, drawing his great lance, he pierced the dragon's mouth and throat. The dragon gave a mighty cry and crashed to the ground.

Bahram leaped forward to cut the dragon's belly open. Inside, he found the wild donkey's baby, trembling like a leaf. The dragon had swallowed it in one gulp! Mother and baby rushed toward each other, while Bahram knelt on the ground to give thanks to Allah.

After a while, the mother donkey nudged Bahram to follow her inside the cave. There she showed him a dozen big jars in which gold, silver and precious jewels lay shining in the dark, untouched by human hands. Bahram had never seen so many riches in his life. He returned to his palace and called for twenty camels to carry the treasure back to Khavarnaq. He sent ten camel loads to his father in Persia and ten to King Nu'man to thank him for all that he had done for him, keeping very little for himself.

One evening, when Bahram had returned from a hunt, he noticed a secret room in his palace that he had never seen before.

"Why have I never been shown this room?" he asked the keeper. "Let me see what's in it. Open the door at once!"

The door was unlocked to reveal a richly painted room, every surface covered with intricate patterns and mosaics. On its walls hung portraits of seven beautiful princesses. They came from India, China, Russia and Greece; from Arabia, Persia and Morocco. Their names were written under their pictures and inscribed under them all, in big gold letters, was his own name. Each princess seemed to smile warmly at him, as if she had known him forever.

"I wonder what all this means?" Bahram asked himself. "Why is my name written here? One day I hope to meet them, for it seems to me that there is a lot to learn from these princesses!"

With these thoughts in mind, Bahram ordered the keeper to lock up the portrait room once more. Not a single soul was to be allowed in. It was now Bahram's mission to find out more about the mysterious princesses.

But before all this could happen, Bahram had to prove himself to be worthy of becoming shah. The occasion soon arose.

When Bahram's father, Shah Yazdigird, died, the noble families of Persia did not want Bahram to succeed him. They were suspicious of his foreign upbringing, so they crowned an old nobleman Shah of Persia instead.

When Bahram heard the news, he was furious. "The throne is mine!" he thundered and at once raised a mighty army of the best swordsmen in Yemen. The army marched, banging their drums, right up to the palace of the new Shah of Persia.

Nobles and generals met Bahram and told him not to waste his time. "The throne is not yours any more. Go back to where you came from."

Bahram answered, "I know I am young and you do not know me, but give me a chance to show that I am worthy. I promise to serve my people well, to be fair to them and protect them. I will not take what is not mine, neither house, nor money, nor land. I will act in fear of Allah and be the best ruler Persia has ever known."

The noblemen were impressed by this speech. They whispered for a while to each other, then the eldest among them stood up and answered, "Bahram, we are pleased to have you back. Your words are wise and have touched our hearts. We know that by right this throne is yours, but you must prove it by deed."

"Very well," said Bahram boldly. "Let the shah meet me tomorrow in the market place. Bring two lions that have not eaten and place the crown of Persia between them. Whoever seizes the crown first from the jaws of the hungry lions will be the true shah of this land."

The noblemen returned to court and told the shah of Bahram's challenge. The shah replied, "It is better to live below the throne than to be killed by lions. I am too old to fight new battles; a young shah is better than an old one. You must give Bahram the throne and not divide the kingdom."

"Your words are wise, O Shah; that is why we chose you. However, we suggest you let Bahram fight the lions, for who knows what may happen."

"Very well, then," the shah replied. "Let us see what tomorrow may bring." The next day a huge crowd assembled to watch the contest. Bahram boldly stepped into the middle of the market place. He had killed a hundred lions, so was not afraid of two. Like the south wind, he raced toward them, shouting at the top of his voice. For a split second, the lions were taken aback and let the crown fall to the ground. Bahram grabbed the golden crown and, holding it aloft, dashed back to the cheering crowd. The lions leaped after him but Bahram drew two arrows from his belt and struck them both through the head. The crowd cheered louder than ever, while the old shah, like the good nobleman he was, warmly embraced Bahram. The young man had won!

On that same day, he was crowned Shah of Persia. Bahram mounted the seven-stepped throne, wearing about his waist the seven-eyed belt of office, set with seven jewels each the color of the seven planets.

The Building of the Seven Pavilions

When Bahram became shah, Persia flourished. Everyone praised him for his justice and wisdom. He never boasted, "I took the crown from the lions' jaws," but said instead, "Allah's hand is mightier than the sword. And since I took the throne with Allah's consent, I will do everything He says."

He asked the nobles in his land to be honest and truthful and never take advantage of their power. He helped the poor and listened to their problems. Wherever he went, markets would bustle and towns prosper.

Then winter came. The crows chased the nightingales away and the bitter cold forced everyone to hide indoors. Shah Bahram sat in his winter rooms, drinking tea, burning incense and huddling by the fire. The seven portraits hanging in the locked room in Khavarnaq were haunting him day and night.

"I must meet these princesses," he thought to himself. "I must invite them here one day."

"What shall I do to make their visit special?" he asked his prime minister.

"Have a palace built for them by Shida," said the Grand Vizier.

"Who is this Shida?" asked Bahram in surprise.

"Do you remember Simnar, the man who built Khavarnaq? Well, Shida is his apprentice," said the Grand Vizier.

"What is so special about him?" asked Bahram.

"He is a master builder and a painter. He uses his chisel like a brush. Geometry, physics and astronomy are like wax in his hands. He really has a special touch."

"Send for him immediately!" Bahram ordered, feeling quite excited about meeting such a talented architect.

Shida arrived at court dressed in golden robes. He kissed the shah's hand and sat by his feet, listening to Bahram as he made his request. After some careful thought, he told the shah, "Your Majesty, I believe I know exactly what to do to make you happy."

"Tell me now!" the shah ordered.

"Sire, I know the sky and stars as well as my home and garden. To be happy on earth, one must copy the heavens. I propose to build a palace with seven pavilions protected by the seven heavenly planets: Saturn, Jupiter, Mars, Venus, Mercury, the Moon and the Sun. Each pavilion will be a different color, each as beautiful as the next. Each princess may choose to live in one and wear its color, and you will visit her on the day ruled by the appropriate planet."

"What an interesting project!" exclaimed Bahram. And he ordered Shida to draw up plans for the Seven Pavilions. Then he sent his envoys laden with gifts and precious jewels to the seven countries where the princesses lived, inviting them to come and inspect the Seven Pavilions.

It took two years for the pavilions to be finished and for the princesses to arrive from their countries. When they reached the palace, a great feast was held for forty days and forty nights. Afterward each princess was escorted to her pavilion.

Princess Furaq of India wished to live in the Black Pavilion of Saturn, while the Greek princess Humay chose the Yellow Pavilion of the Sun. Princess Pari of Arabia selected the Green Pavilion of the Moon, while the Russian princess Nesrin-Nush decided upon the Red Pavilion of Mars. The Moroccan princess Azaryun chose to live in the Blue Pavilion of Mercury, while the Chinese princess Yaghma-Naz preferred the Sandalwood Pavilion of Jupiter. Last, but not least, the Persian princess Durr-Siti selected the White Pavilion of Venus.

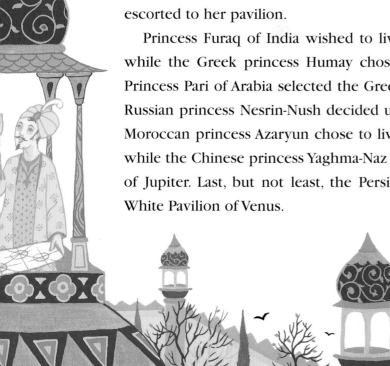

The Raja Who Dressed in Black

Told on Saturday by the Indian Princess

One Saturday, just before sunrise, while the sky was still dark, Shah Bahram put on a black robe, a black turban and black shoes and went to visit the Black Pavilion of Saturn where the Indian princess, Furaq, lived.

"Welcome, great shah," said the black-eyed princess with a smile. She bowed to him, her long black hair touching the hem of her black skirt.

Holding his hand, Princess Furaq led him to a sitting room furnished entirely in black silk. They sat on black cushions, drank licorice tea and ate sweet black figs.

"Tell me why you chose to live in the Black Pavilion," said the shah, "and why you are drawn to the color black. That is a story I would like to hear."

"It is a long one," the princess sighed. "And sad too, Your Majesty."

"Even so, I would really like to hear it," Shah Bahram said.

"Just sit back and relax," said Princess Furaq, pouring him more tea, "and I will begin."

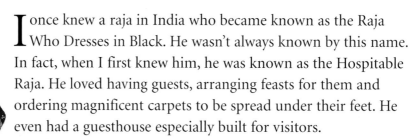

I once knew a raja in India who became known as the Raja Who Dresses in Black. He wasn't always known by this name. In fact, when I first knew him, he was known as the Hospitable Raja. He loved having guests, arranging feasts for them and ordering magnificent carpets to be spread under their feet. He even had a guesthouse especially built for visitors.

After his guests had eaten and drunk their fill, the raja used to see them one by one and ask each of them about their lives, their adventures and the countries they came from. Each guest had to choose a special adventure to tell the raja. Hearing these stories made the raja the happiest and most hospitable raja the world had ever known. To show how happy he was, the raja always dressed in red and yellow.

For years and years the raja lived in this way, ruling his kingdom, entertaining his guests and hearing their wonderful tales, until one morning, just before his meeting with the first guest of the day, the raja disappeared, slipping away in secret from the palace.

His servants searched everywhere for him: in the gardens, in the throne room, in the treasury, in the bedroom, on the palace roof. There was no sign of the raja anywhere. They questioned his counselors and his viziers, but no one knew where he had gone.

A year later, the raja reappeared just as suddenly, looking very sad. Gone was his happy smile, and gone were his red and yellow robes, his bright turbans and colorful crown. Instead, from head to toe, he was dressed completely in black.

While he continued ruling wisely, the raja ordered his guesthouse to be closed and no longer invited visitors. No more banquets were prepared or carpets spread out. There was no more fun, no tales and no laughter.

Puzzled by this sudden change, I went to the raja one day and asked, "Sire, why do you always wear black? Why don't you invite anyone to your guesthouse any more?"

The raja smiled sadly and said, "This is my story. Listen to it and learn."

~

One day, a stranger came to my guesthouse dressed in black from head to toe, just as I am now. From guest to guest I went, listening to their stories, but, when the man in black's turn came, he simply refused to say anything.

"Why are your clothes all black?" I asked.

"I do not wish to talk about it, Your Majesty," he politely replied.

"But tell me, do!" I begged.

"You must excuse me, Sire," he answered. "No one knows the secret of black except for those who wear only black themselves."

"Tell me your secret, then," I pressed.

He again excused himself.

I tried so hard that, in the end, seeing my disappointment, the man finally explained, "Far away in China is a city called the City of the Stupefied. Its people are pale as the moon and their clothes are as black as the sky on a starless night. Whoever visits this city ends up wearing black. More than that I cannot tell. If you will excuse me now, Sire, I must leave." So saying, the man stood up and left.

I was now more puzzled than ever. I could not sleep, I could not eat, I could not concentrate on anything. All I could think of was the City of the Stupefied and the secret of the color black. So I decided to look for it there and then.

I did not tell anyone about my decision. I just took a few robes and plenty of jewels and gold, and off I went with my most trusted servants in search of the city where everyone wore black.

Believe it or not, I found it without much difficulty. It was exactly as my guest had described. Its people were clothed in black and their faces were as white as milk. I rented a house, and for a whole year looked for one person who could tell me the secret of black, but no one said a word.

Then one day I met a butcher who seemed so nice and jolly that I decided to make friends with him. "He will tell me the secret of the city," I told myself. "I will shower him with jewels and gold and win his confidence."

17

So I made friends with the only friendly person in the whole of this sad town. Each day I would offer my friend a new present: a bejeweled dagger, a carved box, a silk turban, a diamond ring. You name it, I gave it.

One evening, my friend the butcher invited me to his house for a feast of delicious meats. He offered me everything my stomach wanted but not what my heart needed. We talked about this and that, but all I desired was to find out the secret of the color black.

Finally my friend said, "Dear stranger, I do not know who you are or why you're here. All I see is a generous heart and a worried face. What do you want from a poor butcher like me? And why did you offer me all your jewelry?"

Touched by his honesty, I told him how I had left my kingdom and my people to discover the secret of black. I told him how I had waited a whole year for someone to tell me why everyone here walked around clad in mourning robes.

The butcher listened to my story without a word. He kept totally silent until I had finished.

"What is the matter, dear man?" I asked. "Have I offended you in any way?"

"You could have asked anything from me, my friend," he replied with tears in his eyes. "My life, my shop, my daughter's hand — anything but the secret of our poor city. But since you have taken so much trouble, I shall do what is possible." Standing up, he took me by the hand and led me to the far end of town.

Not a soul was about. It was pitch dark and I could barely see ahead. Suddenly I bumped into something. It was a large basket attached to a rope that extended far above my head, disappearing into the gloom.

"Climb into it," my friend ordered, helping me inside. "And good luck!"

The moment I stepped into the basket, it moved upward, pulled by the rope. Up and up it went, as if by magic. I was terrified it would never stop, but it did after a while, and I found myself at the top of a very tall column.

Looking down, I saw that I was high up in the sky, quite alone, with nowhere to go. So I waited and waited for something to happen. I waited all night, shivering and frightened.

At dawn, a huge bird alighted near me at the top of the column. Its wings were the size of branches and its feet were like tree roots. Its beak was massive, too, and its feathers covered me like a blanket. The moment it landed on the column, the bird went to sleep.

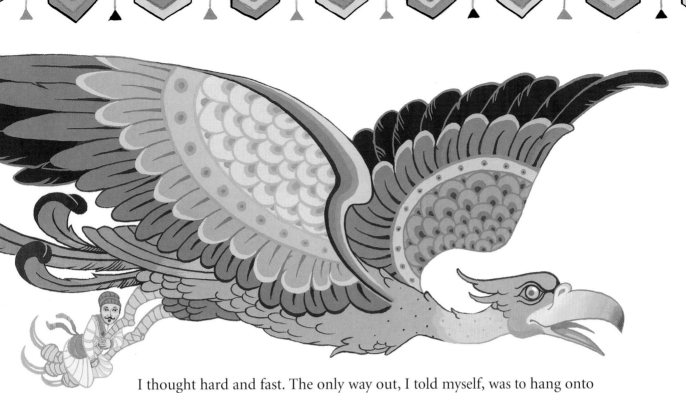

I thought hard and fast. The only way out, I told myself, was to hang onto the bird's feet and fly with it wherever it went. So I waited patiently until it woke up.

Sure enough, at cockcrow, just as the sun appeared, the bird flapped its wings and off it went with me hanging onto its feet. It flew high into the sky, drifting from morning until noon, until, tired from the heat, it searched for shade and cool. It swooped slowly down to earth and landed on grass as soft as silk, covered with flowers that smelled divine, like rosewater or musk.

I quickly let go of the bird's feet and fell gently onto the grass, blessing it a hundred times.

Looking around, lo and behold, I saw a wonderful garden with hundreds of flowers of many kinds. Hyacinths, jasmine and roses grew in a blaze of color among cypress and pine trees. Near a stream, poplar trees waved their branches to dozens of fish shimmering like mercury in the water. The water was turquoise blue, the earth was made of gold dust and the stones were precious jewels. Clearly this was a garden made by houris, close cousins of the fairies. It felt as though I was in paradise.

Around the garden I went, eating its fruits and enjoying its scents, until, tired and happy, I laid my head on the soft grass and drifted into the land of dreams.

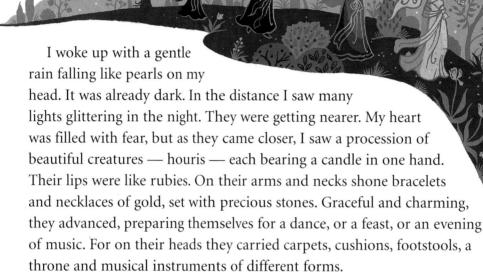

I woke up with a gentle rain falling like pearls on my head. It was already dark. In the distance I saw many lights glittering in the night. They were getting nearer. My heart was filled with fear, but as they came closer, I saw a procession of beautiful creatures — houris — each bearing a candle in one hand. Their lips were like rubies. On their arms and necks shone bracelets and necklaces of gold, set with precious stones. Graceful and charming, they advanced, preparing themselves for a dance, or a feast, or an evening of music. For on their heads they carried carpets, cushions, footstools, a throne and musical instruments of different forms.

"Ah," I told myself, "these houris must have a queen!" And I was right, for there she came, looking as beautiful as the moon on a starry night. She sat on her throne smiling, listening to her companions playing music and watching them dance. After a while, she turned to her nearest friend and said, "Do you sense what I sense? A human is hiding in our garden. Go and bring him here to me."

The lovely houri searched everywhere until she found me hiding behind a tree. She looked surprised, but her only words were, "Arise, the queen of queens awaits you."

I followed her without a word and knelt before the queen, kissing the ground before her feet.

"No need for that, dear man," said the queen, taking my hand. "Come sit beside me and share my meal."

A tray was brought, full of the most delicious food, served in ruby bowls. Whatever I desired appeared immediately on my plate. The cupbearer poured me a heavenly drink that tasted of blackberries and cherries. Then the houris started singing and dancing, playing the harp, flute and tambourine. I leaned toward the queen and asked, "Your Majesty, what is your name, and what is this place called?"

"My name is Turktaz the Beautiful," she answered, "and this is the Kingdom of the Houris where all wishes come true."

"May I wish for a kiss from your beautiful lips?" I asked.

"Not tonight, my friend, not tonight," she replied. "You can kiss any of my maidens, but you will have to wait to kiss me."

Sadly I retreated to my place. I continued to enjoy the music and the graceful dancing of the houris, but my heart was set on stealing a kiss from the lips of the beautiful queen.

Day after day, I walked in the magic garden, enjoying its birds and fruit and dreaming of the evening's pleasures. Night after night, I experienced the same delight and the same torture. I ate the most delicious food, listened to the most beautiful music, watched the most graceful dances, but I was never allowed to kiss the queen.

For twenty-nine nights I asked the queen, "May I kiss you tonight?" And each time she replied, "Impatience is the vice of slaves, my raja. Be patient and you will be rewarded a thousand times." Then she would point at one of her maidens and say, "You can kiss her if you want, but you cannot kiss me yet."

I kissed a new houri every night, but my heart was set on the queen. For nothing is more delicious than forbidden sweets, don't you agree? So although I had the whole of paradise at my feet, I still dreamed of more. How greedy humans can be!

On the thirtieth day, I decided not to take "no" for an answer any longer. I plotted all day on how to get my way with this loveliest of lovelies.

So, when night came and the music started playing and the wine started flowing, I leaned toward the queen and said, "Tonight is the night, my queen, when I shall taste sweet honey from your lips."

She answered, "One more night of patience is all I ask. Tomorrow this treasure shall be yours."

But that night seemed like a year. The food tasted bland, the music sounded dull and my patience was wearing thin.

"Why do I have to wait the whole night?" I asked myself. "What is this talk about impatience being the vice of slaves? I am a raja, not a slave, and rajas are allowed to do whatever they want!"

So, without so much as a "may I" or a "please," I leaned toward the queen and pressed my mouth against her ruby lips, closing my eyes to enjoy them better.

The moment I touched the magic lips without permission, I found myself back in the basket, on top of the column.

I looked down and saw my friend the butcher waving at me. The basket started moving downward and in a few minutes I was in my friend's arms, tears coursing down my cheeks.

"My friend," the butcher said, "don't cry. All the people of the City of the Stupefied have been there before you. That's why we all wear black, to remind ourselves of our impatience and foolishness."

"To lose paradise in a moment of impatience," I replied, "is a sure sign of great folly. Take me back into the city so that I can order some black robes for myself."

In this way, I returned to my kingdom wearing robes of black silk, with sorrow in my heart and in my eyes. I ordered my guesthouse to be shut and gave all my colorful clothes to the poor. From then on, I concentrated on the affairs of my kingdom and became known, no longer as the Hospitable Raja, but as the Raja Who Dresses in Black.

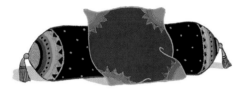

"By the time the raja had finished his tale," said Princess Furaq, "I had decided to dress in black too. For his story had touched me so much, I wanted to share his sorrow.

"If you think about it, black is not only the color of mourning, it is the color of the sky on a dark night. Black is the color of young hair, while the color of old hair is gray. Your pupils — through which you see and learn about the world — are black. And black clothes don't show the dirt, which is why I am wearing black!" said Princess Furaq, giggling.

"Thank you!" said the shah. "Your story will make me dream of black cities, black rajas and black birds."

That night, Shah Bahram laid his head on a black cushion and dreamed of a black moon smiling at him through the window of the Black Pavilion of Saturn.

The Emir Who Did Not Want to Marry

Told on Sunday by the Greek Princess

One Sunday morning, Shah Bahram woke up smiling. The sun was shining, the birds were singing and he was eager to visit the beautiful Humay, the Greek princess who lived in the Yellow Pavilion of the Sun.

Bahram put on a robe of yellow silk, a gold crown and an amber ring. He fastened his golden dagger onto his gold belt and off he went whistling a happy tune.

Princess Humay was as fair as the sun. Her hair was golden and her eyes were like honey. She wore a yellow dress woven with gold threads and a crown made of yellow roses. Sweet amber musk was her perfume. Smiling, she invited the shah to take a seat on a gold couch covered with gold cushions.

"Welcome to the Pavilion of the Sun," said Princess Humay, bringing Shah Bahram white wine in a golden cup.

"Thank you, my lady," said the shah, sipping his wine and tasting a piece of saffron cake that she offered him. "This cake is as sweet as honey and this wine as fragrant as musk," he added, brushing the crumbs off his hand.

Feeling satisfied and refreshed, the shah asked, "What story will you tell me today? Why, for instance, did you decide to live in the Yellow Pavilion, and why do you love the color yellow? Do tell me."

So the princess began her story.

Once upon a time, in the city of Baghdad, there lived a rich emir, so rich he could not count his money. He was handsome, too, as handsome as a spring morning. And he had everything his heart desired: sumptuous palaces, thoroughbred horses, rich carpets, finely wrought swords. He had all except one thing. He had no wife, nor did he want one.

"This is strange," interrupted Bahram. "Such a rich and handsome man, and no wife? No children to give his money to?"

"Well, he was simply terrified of getting married," answered Humay, "and all because of what the best astrologers in the kingdom had foretold when he was young."

The moment the astrologers had finished drawing his horoscope, they all agreed on one point: that the emir should never marry because, if he did, he would spend his life fighting with his wife.

Upon hearing the grim news, the emir decided there and then never to marry for he liked his peace and quiet. For many years, he remained single until, one day, he could stand it no longer.

Summoning his chief servant, the emir asked him to go to the slave market and choose him the most beautiful slave girl he could find there.

For the first few days, the emir was happy with his new companion. But after a week or two, she changed totally. From being modest, patient and kind, she became rude, impatient and greedy. She would start ordering the servants around, demanding expensive clothes and more and more jewels. She became lazy and grouchy. So the emir sent her back to the slave merchant, asking for a new girl to be sent.

One after another, slave girls came and went. Month after month, the emir looked in vain for that rare pearl, a woman who would be loving, patient and kind, not only to him but to everyone she met, a woman who would not argue, shout and order everyone around, demanding jewelry, gowns and even whole towns to be given to her!

What was the reason for all this bad luck, you may ask. Why was the emir lonely and never satisfied? The reason is not too difficult to find.

Hidden in the remotest room of the castle was an old servant woman, toothless and ugly, with a hunched back and a nasty heart. She disliked the emir and tried to harm him at every opportunity. Every morning, while the emir was busy with his viziers, she went secretly to his favorite slave girl and started putting ideas into her head.

"You should be treated like a queen, not a slave," she would whisper under her bad breath. "You should ask for a new dress today," she would say, hissing through her toothless gums. "You should demand diamonds and rubies, and pearl necklaces."

No wonder the slave girls became greedy! No wonder nothing would please them! And no wonder the emir got rid of them all!

At last, the emir grew weary. He retired to his river palace and told his chief servant, "Do not bring me any more slave girls."

So, for a while, the emir was alone again. He would spend his days wandering by the riverside, dreaming of a loving and patient wife.

One morning, the chief servant came running to the breakfast room, shouting, "I've found her! I've found her!"

"You've found whom?" asked the emir, munching on his date cake.

"The perfect girl, Your Majesty," answered the chief servant with a bow.

"Who is she?" asked the emir, taking a sip of his chamomile tea.

"She has come with a slave caravan all the way from China," said the chief servant excitedly. "Her hair is as black as the night and her face as pale as the moon. She can sing, dance, recite poetry and play the harp. And she has the sweetest of tempers," he added quickly.

"I do not want anyone," said the emir, rinsing his hands with rosewater. "I doubt that she will be any different from the rest."

"Oh, Majesty, please consider her, just this time, this last time!" begged the chief servant.

"All right, all right," mumbled the emir, drying his hands with a silk cloth. "Bring her to me. But this is the last time I give in to your advice."

The slave merchant was summoned at once to the palace with the girl, and when the emir saw her, he fell instantly in love.

"I will take her," he said to the slave merchant.

"I am sorry, Sire, but I cannot give her away," the merchant answered.

"Why not?" asked the emir.

"This Chinese beauty for whom your heart beats has been bought by all the

kings of the Orient. Each time I sold her she was returned to me the very next day," the merchant explained. "No one would say why."

"I will take her anyway," the emir declared. "I welcome challenges," he added, throwing a purse full of gold at the bewildered merchant.

The next morning, the merchant waited for the emir to send the slave girl back, but he did not. The following morning, the merchant waited again and the morning after too. Finally, tired of waiting, the merchant took his leave, hoping the slave girl had passed the test.

She had indeed charmed his Majesty in every way. Whatever she did — dance, sing or play the harp — she did perfectly. She worked like a slave but behaved like a queen: patient, loving and kind. The sly words of the evil old servant woman had no effect on her. She never asked the emir for money, jewels or clothing, but followed the emir like his shadow, always faithful and quiet. The emir was conquered by her and proposed marriage. The court could not believe it. Then, to everyone's surprise, she politely refused. The court was stunned.

"How dare she say 'no' to our emir," they whispered. "Who does she think she is?"

The emir surprised them even more by not getting angry at all. Instead he invited the lovely slave to a candlelit dinner by the riverside. After eating an exquisite meal and listening to enchanting music and wonderful songs, the emir said, "Tell me, beautiful one, why you refused to marry me?"

Blushing under her veil, the slave girl answered, "My lord, you are my emir and master, but I am unable to tell you the truth."

"The truth must never be hidden," argued the emir. "Let me tell you this story."

King Solomon had a beautiful wife called Bilqis, whom he loved and respected. In addition, he had everything a king could ask for: fame, wisdom and riches. But, alas, his only son was born crippled in hand and foot, unable to lift a piece of bread to his mouth or walk a single step without help.

"O King," said Bilqis, "both of us have perfectly formed hands and feet. Why is our son so crippled? Something has to be done. I beg you, dear husband, to pray to God for guidance."

King Solomon prayed with all his heart, asking God for an answer to his problem. That night, the angel Gabriel appeared to him in a dream and said, "If you and Bilqis were to speak the truth to each other, your child would be cured."

In the morning, King Solomon hurried to his wife and told her, "My dear, all is clear. The cure will happen when we speak the truth to each other."

"The truth, what truth?" asked Bilqis in surprise.

"The truth we have been hiding from each other all these years," King Solomon answered.

Queen Bilqis took a deep breath, summoned her courage and said, "The truth, my lord, is that you are a wonderful king and husband, loved and respected by all. But I, your queen, have to confess that whenever I see a handsome man, my heart beats faster and I start wishing he were my husband instead."

The moment Queen Bilqis spoke the truth, the little prince stretched his arms and said, "Look, Mother, I can hold your hand now!"

So overjoyed was he by the miracle, that King Solomon could not be angry with Bilqis. Instead, summoning his courage in turn, he bowed his head and told her, "When people come to me seeking words of wisdom, the first thing I do is look at the gift they are carrying in their hands. I feel ashamed of my greed, for God has blessed me beyond belief. But I cannot help it."

The moment King Solomon spoke the truth, the little prince stretched his legs, stood on his feet and said, "See, Father, I can walk. I don't need crutches any more!"

Solomon and Bilqis embraced their son with tears in their eyes and promised from then on always to tell the truth, however painful it might seem at first.

When the emir had finished his story, he looked into the slave girl's eyes and said, "If Solomon and Bilqis could tell each other the truth, my love, maybe you can too."

The slave girl looked at him through her veil and saw only gentleness and concern. She decided to trust him, for a secret shared is lighter to bear.

"If I tell you my secret, Your Majesty, will you tell me yours? Will you tell me why hundreds of slave girls have come and gone, and yet you have given your heart to none of them?"

"Tell me yours first, my dear, then I shall tell you mine," the emir promised.

"My secret, my lord, is a sad one to share. All the women in my family die at childbirth. That is why I made a vow never to marry, for I prefer to live single and have no worry."

"Your secret is sad indeed," replied the emir. "But it sleeps safely in my heart."

"Now that I have revealed my secret," said the slave girl, "it is your turn, Majesty, to unveil the mystery of the hundred slave girls who came and went through these palace gates."

"Some years ago those who study the planets and the stars and draw the maps of people's hearts and fates told me that if I ever married, I would spend my life fighting with my wife. Many a woman I had brought to me, wishing to make her my queen. But the moment she set her eyes on splendor and wealth, she became greedy, impatient and unkind. You alone, my love, have remained pure of heart, loving, patient and gentle. You alone shall be my queen," declared the emir, kissing the slave girl's hands.

"Your Majesty's words are music to my soul," replied the girl. "Let us promise each other, with the rising sun as our witness, that the truth shall be our fortress, so that what we most fear may never come to pass."

"Come here, my chosen one. Take off your silken veil so I can admire your beauty. For no emir before me has been blessed with a companion as precious as you."

The sun showered its golden rays on the emir and his bride, who embraced and kissed and promised always to keep the truth in their marriage as guide.

"Yellow makes people happy," said Princess Humay, finishing her story. "It is the color of saffron, gold and good advice, and it is the color of truth. The sun is like a golden ball, and the wheat in summer is yellow. Lemons, pears and apples are yellow, and so is white wine in a golden cup."

"Thank you for such a fascinating story," said Shah Bahram to Princess Humay. "This day that I have spent in the Yellow Pavilion of the Sun will remain as precious as gold!"

The Lovesick Hermit

Told on Monday by the Arabian Princess

One Monday, Shah Bahram dressed in a green robe, a green turban and a green coat and walked through the meadows carrying a green parasol. Toward the emerald pavilion he went, whistling a merry tune. The grass beneath his feet danced and the flowers waved their heads. Birds joined in the song and butterflies and bees drifted by.

In the garden of the Green Pavilion of the Moon stood Princess Pari, from Arabia. Her jade bracelets made a lovely tinkling sound and her emerald-studded crown shone in the sunlight.

"Welcome to the Green Pavilion of the Moon," said Princess Pari, her green gown swishing around her like a wheat field in the breeze. "Would Your Majesty like some mint tea?" she asked, showing the shah in.

Lunch was served to music. A lute player and a drummer played some haunting melodies from the desert, while the shah and the princess ate lamb and peas, followed by green beans with almonds, and pistachios, greengages and grapes for dessert.

As they walked in the garden, Shah Bahram said, "What story will you tell me today? Will you explain why you selected the Green Pavilion, and why the color green is so special to you?"

Seated under the shade of the cypress tree, Princess Pari began her story.

In the kingdom of Byzantium lived a gentleman as sweet as honey and as pure and kind as a dove. Bishr lived by himself, devoting his life to prayer and to God, eating only dry bread and fruit and working the land.

He barely saw anyone. Twice a year he took his produce to the market, and sat in front of his baskets waiting for people to buy. Even then he rarely talked, merely smiling gently as people put their money in his skinny hand.

But one day, as he sat by his baskets, something strange happened to him. A tall woman dressed all in black came to buy some fruit from his stall. As she picked up her basket, and with the help of a gentle breeze, her veil was lifted off her face for a few seconds and Bishr caught sight of the most beautiful face he had ever seen, almond eyes shining like emeralds and lips bright as rubies.

His heart beat faster and his breath grew shorter. "What is happening to me?" Bishr asked himself. "Is this what people call love?"

He brushed the idea away like a bothersome fly and went on smiling gently as he finished selling his fruit. But like a persistent wasp, the image of this beautiful woman kept on buzzing around his head.

"I must pack up and pray," Bishr said to himself. "This is getting out of hand."

He said his evening prayers and his morning ones, but he still could not banish those emerald-green eyes from his mind. "This is getting dangerous," said the poor hermit to himself. "I must leave immediately and go on a pilgrimage to the Holy Land."

That same day, Bishr bundled up his meager possessions and left for Jerusalem, praying to God to deliver him from distracting visions.

In Jerusalem he prayed hard for God to purify his heart. After touring the holy shrines, Bishr felt at peace with himself at last and with the world around him.

On his return journey, Bishr met a man from the town near his home, and they traveled together. The man talked nonstop, criticizing the ignorance of everyone, including the poor hermit, and boasting of his superior knowledge.

"What is your name, poor man?" he began by asking.

"It is Bishr, sir," answered the hermit.

"Bishr means 'good news,'" said the man. "But what good do you bring to people, you hermits?"

"All that is good comes from God," replied Bishr. "I am only his servant."

"I am Malikha, chief of the learned," said the man. "I know all about the stars and the planets. I know the secrets of the heavens, although I've never been so high. Anything happening in the world, I see as sharply as a sword. I can turn stones into gems, amber into rubies and sand into gold."

"Goodness!" exclaimed Bishr, amazed at these boastful words.

"Tell me, dear man," continued Malikha without a pause, "why this cloud is as black as smoke and that one as white as milk?"

"It is God who made them so," replied the hermit.

"Tell me, then, why this mountain is higher than its sister?"

"It is God who chose it to be so," said Bishr patiently.

"Haven't you heard of condensation or erosion, you ignorant fellow?" Malikha shouted.

"I am not ignorant," answered Bishr calmly. "I just see the work of God's hand in everything."

Malikha talked without pausing for breath, through every desert and mountain pass. He had something to say about everything. Poor Bishr's head was soon bursting with the nonstop chatter and constant boasting.

After days of sun, they finally reached some shade. A sturdy tree spread its branches lush and green against the sky. On the grass beneath it, a huge jar full of clear water was buried up to its neck.

"I wonder who buried this jar up to its brim?" asked Malikha.

"It must be a kind soul who thought of thirsty travelers," answered Bishr.

"Nonsense," argued Malikha. "It must be a hunter's trap for goats, wild donkeys or gazelles. While the animal is drinking from the jar, the hunter kills it. Yes, that must be it," concluded Malikha, proud of his logic.

"Why do you always have such unpleasant thoughts?" asked Bishr. "If you always think of bad things, they will happen to you. And if you always believe others to be evil, take a look first at your own heart."

With these words, Bishr knelt down and drank of the water in the jar, then rested under the tree, enjoying its welcoming shade.

Copying Bishr, Malikha drank the water also. But instead of resting under the tree, he started to take his clothes off.

"What are you doing, my friend?" cried Bishr.

"Just having a wash," replied Malikha.

"This water is for drinking and not for washing," said Bishr, getting angry. "Why should you spoil for others what you have enjoyed yourself? How can people drink water dirtied by your sweat?"

"Move away!" said Malikha, continuing to undress. "I shall do whatever I please." With these words, he jumped into the huge jar.

Alas, the jar was not in fact a jar, but a well, and a deep one too. Moreover, Malikha did not know how to swim, so he drowned and sank deep into the dark hole.

Bishr was stunned. It had all happened so fast. It is true he did not like Malikha, but he did not wish him dead. He shed a few tears for the poor man's soul and a few more for the pollution his body was causing the well. He then said some prayers for the dead and gathered his companion's clothes to take them to his family.

As he picked up Malikha's robes, his linen turban and his silk belt, Bishr came across a box, fastened with a lock. Finding the key, he opened it, hoping to discover something that would tell him about the dead man's kin. Imagine what he found instead: a thousand golden coins from ancient Egypt!

"Goodness!" exclaimed Bishr with delight. "What treasure! If I take it home, everyone will be amazed and wonder how I became rich when I spend my days in prayers and silence."

But then a little voice rose in his head telling him not to steal a dead man's treasure, for stealing does not bring happiness. So Bishr fastened the box again and went along the road, feeling tired and old.

All along the way back home, Bishr argued with the voice that told him, "You have no choice but to be good and honest. One does not betray a friend, especially after he is dead. If you did that, what sort of person would you be?"

At last Bishr reached the town near his home. Showing Malikha's clothing to all he met, he asked, "Do you know where the owner of these clothes might have lived?"

Finally one person answered, "Walk on a little until you reach the seventh house at the end of the road. It looks like a mansion. It is said that a man named Malikha lived there."

Carrying Malikha's clothes and gold, Bishr walked on a little until he arrived at the house and knocked on the door. A tall, veiled woman with green eyes opened the door and welcomed him in.

"What brings you to this home, holy man?" she asked the hermit.

"It is a long story that cannot be told on a doorstep," Bishr answered.

"Then please come in and give your dusty feet a rest," the young woman replied.

She summoned a servant to bring sorbet and sweet cakes for the hermit and sat on a cushion to listen to his tale.

Bishr told the lady the whole story of his meeting with Malikha. He mentioned the man's constant boasting and chatter and his strong opinions on every topic. He then told the woman about the sad death of his companion who thought the well a jar and would not listen to his objections about washing in it.

"May I lay at your feet Malikha's clothing and his gold?" Bishr finally said.

Touched by the hermit's honesty, the woman revealed her true identity. "I am Malikha's wife," she said. "I know all about his tantrums and boastful, overbearing ways. For years I prayed to God to change my husband's heart and spare me from his cruelty. But, praise be to God, who decided differently. I am now free and rich, all because of your honesty."

"I am God's humble servant," Bishr replied. "I only did what He required. He who only thinks of gold, forgetting friends, family and guests, will pay for it a thousandfold, not in this world but in the next."

With these words, Bishr handed the gold to Malikha's wife, who could not stop crying at the sight of all this money that Bishr's honesty had forbidden him to keep for himself.

"I have never met a man as kind or as honest as you," she said, wiping her beautiful eyes with a green handkerchief. "Will you do me the honor of becoming my husband?"

Not waiting for Bishr to answer, she lifted the veil from her face. There, staring at him, were the almond-shaped eyes shining like emeralds and the lips bright as rubies.

Bishr could not believe his eyes, or his luck. Was it a dream or a mirage, he asked himself. Was she indeed the woman he had seen at the market and whom he had tried to run away from?

Many different thoughts raced through his head. At this moment, feelings of joy mingled with those of guilt.

"Decisions, decisions. I must make one," he told himself. "How can I go back to being a simple hermit when God is offering me such a lovely bride to be my companion for life — someone to love and cherish and grow old with?"

The fear of growing old alone was the one that finally won. Having reached his decision, Bishr suddenly felt younger and happier than he had in a long time.

"He is lucky who has found the woman of his dreams," said the hermit, kissing the lady's hand. "I have longed to meet you since that day when your veil lifted to show me your face. Your emerald-green eyes have haunted me for days and nights, and many a time in my dreams I have kissed your ruby lips."

"You can kiss them now if you want," she said shyly.

So, for the first time in his life, Bishr kissed a woman's lips. He felt he was in paradise, growing wings and flying high, for he had found his angel on earth. It was in green robes that both were married, for green is the color of new life. It is the color of hope and joy and the sacred color of their faith. Green is the color of healthy corn growing in the fields. It is the color worn by many angels in paradise. Green is the favorite color of children, for it makes their souls happy and their eyes rejoice.

Her story finished, Princess Pari smiled at Shah Bahram with her green eyes. The princess asked her maid to draw the green curtains and bring a green cover for the shah. Then, with a tinkling of her jade bracelets, she pulled the cover up over him and left him in the land of dreams, where everything was colored green.

The Princess
of the Fort

Told on Tuesday by the Russian Princess

One dark and rainy Tuesday in the middle of winter, Shah Bahram dressed in red from head to toe and went to visit the Russian princess of the Red Pavilion of Mars.

The shah was in a very good mood because it was his name day. Being Tuesday, it was also the day of Mars, the god of war. Bahram wanted very much to be compared to Mars because he always won his battles.

So it was with joy in his heart that Shah Bahram entered the Red Pavilion. He was greeted by Princess Nesrin-Nush, daughter of the Russian czar, wearing a red velvet gown, red slippers and a garnet-encrusted crown.

"Welcome to the Red Pavilion of Mars, my lord," said Nesrin-Nush, seating the shah in front of a roaring fire. "Would you care for a cup of red wine, with some cherries and strawberries in syrup?"

"Nothing better than wine to warm the blood on a cold winter day," answered the shah, helping himself to the fruit. "Delicious, delicious," he muttered, licking the syrup off his lips.

"Will you tell me a special story for my name day?" he asked eagerly. "There is nothing nicer than listening to a story in front of a roaring fire on a dark rainy day. I would love to know why you chose to live in the Red Pavilion, and why you so adore the color red. Can you tell me?"

Princess Nesrin-Nush blushed. Her cheeks were as red as apples and her hair had a coppery sheen. On her finger, she wore a ruby the size of a cherry. "Very well," she replied. "It is a story that comes all the way from Russia, my home country."

It is about a princess as beautiful as the moon and as tall as a cypress. Her cheeks were the color of roses and her lips were as sweet as sugar. Her hair was jet black and reached to her waist. She was known throughout the kingdom for her beauty and her wisdom.

She had read all the books on magic that had ever been written, and her passion in life was to solve all things hidden. She loved to invent riddles and give them to her friends to solve.

All the princes of that kingdom and the neighboring kingdoms wanted her hand in marriage. Day and night, they swarmed around the palace gates in their carriages, like bees around a hive.

In order to escape these young men, the princess went to hide in a castle on a high mountain. She had a high wall built around it and placed a thousand guards along the wall. These guards were not made of flesh and blood but of iron and stone. Each held a sword in its right hand, ready to strike at any intruder who dared to cross the wall.

There she spent her days studying the stars and the moon and their influence on people's lives and moods. From east to west she was known as the "Princess of the Fort."

The king, her father, did not know what to do with his daughter. How would he ever become a grandfather if his one and only daughter hid like a precious ring in a box, refusing to meet any suitor?

At last the poor king sent his daughter a kind request begging her to change her mind. "Please, please," he said. "I must see you as a bride before I grow too old and die."

The princess's heart softened when she read her father's words. She took her paintbrush in one hand and her paints in the other and went up to the topmost room of one of her towers to paint a portrait of herself wearing a scarlet dress and a ruby-studded crown.

You see, the Princess of the Fort was a wonderful painter who had studied under famous Chinese masters. She was equally good at portraits and landscapes, and would paint for hours on end up in her tower.

When her portrait was finished, she sent it to her father with the following note:

> *Dear Papa,*
>
> *I love you dearly and I don't want you to be upset. Here is what I suggest. Please hang my portrait by the palace gates and underneath it write: "Whoever would like my daughter as a bride has to fulfill four conditions. First of all, he has to be noble, beautiful and tall. Second, he must fight his way through the guards of iron and stone. Third, he must find the fortress door and walk along its corridors. Fourth, he must solve the riddles that she will put to him. If he gives her the right answers, she promises to be his forever. The man who passes all these tests will win her hand. But the man who fails will, alas, lose his head."*
>
> *Your beloved daughter*

The king sighed when he read the message. What could one do with such a clever but wayward daughter? So he sent his messenger with strict instructions to hang his daughter's portrait by the palace gates and fix beneath it her list of conditions.

The news spread like a storm on a wild winter's night. Suitors came from far and wide to try their luck. But, one by one, they succumbed to the guards of iron and stone. Each and every one lost his head trying to pass through the thousand guards. Heads were piled up on top of the fortress wall as a warning to any suitor foolhardy enough to try his luck with the princess.

The whole town shivered. The number of young men throughout the land had dwindled. Mothers begged their sons not to go near the portrait, because the moment they saw it, they were enchanted. But, as you know, young men in love rarely listen to the voice of reason. For them, it would have been treason not to follow the call of their hearts. So off they went to conquer the fortress where the princess lived, but had their heads chopped off instead.

Among the young men who had heard about the beauty of the princess was a handsome prince, clever, strong, courageous and honest. He passed by the palace one day and saw her portrait hanging by the gates. He could not take his eyes off it.

"Is it possible," he asked himself, "to fall in love with a girl you have never met?"

But no matter how hard he tried to forget her eyes, her face, her teasing smile, he simply could not. Each morning and night he passed by the gates and saluted the portrait of his impossible love. He had no wish to be killed and had a feeling there must be a trick behind it all.

"I must go and consult a magician," he said. "I need a great plan, a clever one, a plan that will help me win the love of this woman."

The prince asked everyone he met whether they knew of a magician. They told him, yes, there was a man who lived in a cave on a nearby mountain and knew all the magic secrets there were to know.

"Just climb the mountain," they said, "and you will see him sitting at the mouth of the cave, on the floor, praying or chanting or inventing a new spell."

So off he went, the handsome prince, following the goats and the wind, until he reached the mouth of the cave, where the old sage sat on the floor.

"Good morning, young man," said the old sage. "What brings you to this forsaken spot?"

"Love brings me here," the prince answered. "I have come to learn from you its secrets and its spells."

"Sit down and listen," said the magician. "Love is not an easy thing to master. Are you prepared to sit for days, learning all the different ways to break a spell or make one up, to suit the one you love?"

"Yes, I am," replied the prince.

"Let us start, then," said the old man.

The prince spent days listening to the sage. When he had memorized all that he needed to know, he thanked the magician and went back to the town. There he dressed in red armor and, slinging his drum across his shoulder, told everyone he was embarking on a special war. He said that he was taking revenge for the thousand men who had lost their heads trying to win the hand of the princess.

Up to the high fortress he went, remembering all the spells he had learned and summoning the spirits of the earth. One by one, he fought the guards of iron and stone and broke their swords the moment he said the magic words. When he had overcome the last one, he looked for the entrance to the fort. For this, he used his drum and not his eyes: every few steps, he banged his drum until a hollow sound echoed back from the wall of the fortress.

"Aha!" he said to himself. "That must be the tunnel to the door of the fort. I must dig a hole until I find it."

And that's exactly what he did, the clever prince. Dig, dig, dig went his shovel for hours on end, until he found the entrance to the fort.

The moment he reached the door, a servant was there to welcome him with steaming towels to clean his hands and a cup of tea to warm his heart. The princess, who had followed the prince's progress from start to finish, had sent a message for him. It read:

> Dear Prince,
> I am an admirer of your skills. You managed to achieve what a thousand men failed to work out. Congratulations and well done!
> There is still one condition to fulfill, however. Meet me tomorrow at my father's palace, and I shall give you four riddles to solve on your own. If you succeed, my love for you will be complete. I shall marry you and be loyal to you forever, for in you I will have found an equal.
>
> The Princess of the Fort.

When the prince returned to the town, crowds gathered by the roadside and threw gold coins, rice and rose petals at him. Young girls fell in love with him at first sight and wished he would marry them instead of the Princess of the Fort.

He was welcomed as a champion, for he truly was one.

"Hail to our hero," some shouted. "If the king does not let you marry his daughter, we shall make you our king instead!"

"Yes, yes," agreed the rest. "The king has been too lenient with his daughter. He has let her get away with murder a thousand times."

"Calm down, calm down, my friends," the prince replied. "Let us wait and see what tomorrow brings. I might guess the riddles and the princess will be mine in the morning."

The people went on their way, wondering about the prince's fate. Would he win the princess or be condemned to death like all the others, they asked themselves.

When morning came, the prince donned red velvet pants with a matching shirt, and hung from his belt his golden sword with its ruby-encrusted hilt. He was not afraid of the test, but of meeting the beautiful princess.

Beautiful indeed she was that day, dressed in crimson silk, a ruby-studded crown, with a strand of pearls around her neck.

Her father and his court were waiting in suspense for the four questions that she would ask the prince. Would he or would he not solve the four riddles, they wondered. Would it end in a marriage or a funeral?

At last the prince came in and bowed to the king and to the court.

"I am ready, Sire," he said, "to face the final test."

The princess, hiding behind a curtain, summoned the treasurer of the kingdom. She gave him her pearl earrings and said, "Take them to the prince, then bring back his answer."

The prince looked at the two tiny white balls, weighed them carefully, and asked the treasurer for three more pearls. He then said, "Please take these five pearls to Her Highness."

The princess was pleased with the answer. She then took a stone and crushed the five pearls, adding sugar to them. She asked the treasurer to take the mixture back to the prince.

The prince sniffed the mixture, put a drop on his finger and tasted it.

"Mmm…I see what she means," he muttered. "Treasurer," he called, "bring me a glass of milk."

He stirred the mixture into the milk, making sure there were no lumps.

"Please take this glass to Her Highness," he told the treasurer.

The princess drank the milk, took the ruby ring off her finger and sent it to the prince who immediately put it on. In exchange he gave her a beautiful shiny pearl.

The princess placed the pearl in her palm, took off her necklace and looked for a matching bead. When she had found a pearl the same size as that of the prince's, she removed it from her necklace, placed the pearls side by side and sent them to the prince.

The prince asked the treasurer for a lucky blue bead, tied the two pearls and the blue bead with silk thread and sent them back to the princess.

When the princess saw what the prince had done with her two pearls, she smiled, fastened them around her neck and told her father, "Rejoice, Your Majesty, for I have finally found a man wiser than me."

"I am so glad for you, my child," said the king, breathing a big sigh of relief. "But could you explain to me what exactly went on between you and this handsome one? Old and dumb I may be, but your hidden messages escaped me."

"It is very simple," the princess answered. "When I took off my pearl earrings and gave them to him, I was saying: Life is as beautiful as a pearl but as short as two days — for earrings are always a pair. When he added three pearls to my pair, he was answering: I agree that life passes quickly, but it seems longer than two days and more like five.

"When I added sugar to the pearls and ground them together, I was saying: Life is bitter and sweet at the same time. He agreed with me but said that one had no choice but to drink from the bittersweet cup of life. That is why he mixed the sugar and the pearl powder with the milk and gave it to me to drink.

"After I had drunk the milk, I gave him my ruby ring, indicating that I accepted him as my husband. When he placed the ring on his finger, he was telling me that he accepted my offer.

"When he then gave me a pearl, he was saying: You are a very precious and rare pearl. When I found another pearl to equal his, I was saying: You are a rare pearl too.

"When he joined both pearls to the blue bead, he was saying: I hope that our marriage will be lucky.

"When I wore the necklace he gave me, I was telling him: You are the only one for me."

The king was so pleased to see his daughter happy that he invited the whole town to the wedding. The people feasted for forty days and forty nights. The clever prince and his Russian princess lived in love and happiness for a long, long time.

On the day he set out to solve the four riddles, the prince had dressed in red to bring him luck. From that day on, the prince wore only red: for work and for pleasure, in winter and in summer. His bedroom was red, his dining room was red and his living room, too.

His love of red was so well known that he became known as the Prince of Red.

Red is the color of precious gems like ruby, garnet and carnelian. Red is the color of blood and life, and red cheeks are a sign of good health. Red roses are queens of the garden and the delight of lovers. Red is the color of passion, of warm fires and of pomegranates.

"Red is also my favorite color, which is why this pavilion is red," said Nesrin-Nush, concluding her story.

"Red is the color of your lovely cheeks," said Bahram. "It is the color of my favorite wine, and of your ruby ring."

Princess Nesrin-Nush blushed with happiness and the heady smell of tea roses filled the room.

"I shall dream of strange adventures tonight, of fortresses and dark tunnels, guards and strange riddles," Shah Bahram yawned.

"Then it is high time you went to bed," whispered Nesrin-Nush. "It is almost dawn. Look: the sky is already tinged with red!"

The Adventures of Young Mahan

Told on Wednesday by the Moroccan Princess

One Wednesday morning, when the sky was turquoise blue and the air as crisp and clean as a new silk robe, Shah Bahram awoke from a dream of blue birds swooping over a blue sea, feeling as light as a feather.

He hummed a happy tune as he ate his breakfast on blue china, then he dressed in blue pants, tying his turquoise belt over a matching shirt.

"What a glorious day," he told his servant, as he pinned a sapphire on his turban. "Please prepare my horse Sultan, for today we shall visit the Morrocan Princess of the Blue Pavilion."

Princess Azaryun's eyes were as blue as a lake and her hair as dark as the night. She spoke several languages and sang as sweetly as a lark on a summer morning. Sapphires and diamonds adorned her neck, and small turquoises were sewn onto her dress.

"Welcome to the Blue Pavilion of Mercury, Your Majesty," said the princess, smiling. "Please come in. We usually play music in the morning."

"Perfect," answered the shah. "Music is a wonderful art."

So they both sat down and listened to lute and flute, drums and harp.

"Will you tell me why you wanted to live in the Blue Pavilion and why blue means so much to you?" Shah Bahram asked. "I'd like to hear your story."

"Very well," replied Azaryun. "I shall tell you."

Mahan was a young man from Egypt, as handsome and slender as a new moon, and born with a silver spoon in his mouth. He was popular with his friends, his coffers were always full of gold. Yet he never seemed to do a stroke of work, but spent his time going to one party after another.

One evening, he was at one of these parties, trying all sorts of food, drinking all kinds of wine, enjoying a few games and listening to a few songs. The moon that night was as bright as the day. The young men told stories, danced and sang to their heart's delight.

Feeling flushed with all the wine, Mahan took a walk under the palm trees, enjoying the cool breeze. He walked for a while, not noticing he was getting further and further away from the crowd. Lost in thought, he kept asking himself questions like: "What is the purpose of life? Why, when I was born so lucky, rich and bright, do so many people live in poverty and misery?"

Suddenly he noticed a figure in the distance waving to him like a long-lost friend. Mahan, drawing nearer, thought he must be a late arrival for the party. "Why have you come so late, my friend?" he asked.

"I had urgent business with someone in town but, when I arrived, the gates were closed. It was too late to go home, so I decided to come to see you instead," the stranger replied.

"What kind of business is done at night?" asked Mahan in a fearful voice.

"The type of business that pays no taxes," the stranger answered. "There is a village chief who wants to sell us his sheep half price. If we take them to the market tomorrow morning, we will double our profit without doing a thing."

"It sounds good to me," said Mahan, excited at the thought of making money so easily.

"Then follow me," said the stranger.

"Do you know what happens when one follows strangers?"
Princess Azaryun asked.

"One gets into trouble sooner or later," Shah Bahram replied.

Poor Mahan walked for miles on end, following his so-called friend. The city gates had disappeared from sight, and it was almost daylight. The Nile, which was supposedly nearby, was nowhere to be seen.

"I must have really been drunk last night, to think I was only a mile away from the river," Mahan thought to himself.

Still, he asked no questions, following the stranger blindly until the sun rose. Mahan watched it rise, then turned to ask his friend how much longer they would be and whether this walk would ever end. But his friend had suddenly disappeared, like a mirage or a drawing in the sand. Mahan shouted, looked everywhere, even cried a little, but he was all alone, standing in the desert like a lost fawn.

"Was this person real, or did I see him in my dream?" he kept asking himself. "What will happen to me?" he sobbed. "No one will ever find me!"

Feeling very upset, he lay down on the sand to rest his weary feet. As the sun rose high in the sky and beat down on his head, he stood up and slowly started walking, the strength gone from his legs. With neither food nor drink, he soon felt sick and weak. Finally, as night drew in, he spotted a cave. To his tired eyes, the blades of dry grass around it seemed to wriggle like small snakes. He dashed past them into the cave where, huddled in a corner, he closed his eyes and fell at once into a deep slumber.

Mahan slept all night and throughout the following day, only waking when he heard the sound of voices. He opened one eye, then the other, his arms still wrapped around his shoulders. Outside the cave, two people were passing by in the dusk: a man and a woman, heavily laden with bundles on their backs.

As they drew closer, Mahan shouted for joy, "Dear people, stop! Can't you see I am a fellow-traveler who has lost his way?"

"Who are you?" asked the man.

"I am Mahan the Clever," answered Mahan. "But I am lost in the desert and need help right now."

"Where are you from, young man?" the woman asked. "Where is your family and why are you lost?"

When Mahan explained what had befallen him, the man exclaimed, "Didn't you know that you are in demon country, full of ghouls and wicked beasts?"

"No, I didn't," answered Mahan sheepishly. "Could you please lead me out of this wilderness and into safety?"

"We shall," the man promised. "You don't realize how lucky you are, young man! You have just escaped death by a hair's breadth! The stranger you followed was none other than a horrible demon called Hayil, known as the Terror of the Desert. Hundreds like you have been led astray by him. You should be glad that we have come your way. My wife and I shall lead you in safety to the first gate of the city."

Mahan thanked God for sending him these two guides to lead him through the desert. So he followed them, mile after mile, in total silence, not stopping even for a moment. They walked and walked through the night, until the sun began to rise. Then, with a blink of an eyelid, the couple were gone, leaving Mahan all alone once again, totally exhausted and in despair.

"What is happening to me?" he asked himself. "Is this all a bad dream or a new reality?"

With these words, he collapsed, falling to the ground with a thud, and slept for a long time. It was his stomach that woke him, with the noisiest rumbling he had ever heard.

"Be quiet," he said. "I know you haven't eaten anything for days. In a moment I shall look for food to fill you up."

So Mahan spent the day digging for roots and eating whatever seeds and nuts he could find. From hill to hill he climbed, sick of being so lost and blind.

"Why do I always believe what strangers say?" he chided himself. "Maybe I deserve what has happened to me."

As it was getting dark, Mahan started looking around for another cave to hide in, safe from the beasts and the jinns. When at last he found one, he slept really badly, dreaming mostly of demons and wicked fairies.

He awoke to the sound of galloping hooves. Running from the cave, he hid behind some rocks. In the distance he could see a rider, spurring on his horse faster and faster, followed by another horse with no rider. The moment the horses sensed Mahan's presence, they stopped and neighed, the first horse almost throwing its rider to the ground. The man, angry at being stopped in his tracks, looked around and saw Mahan crouching behind a rock.

"Don't move, bandit!" the rider shouted. "Or I will chop off your head!"

"Please, sir," Mahan pleaded. "Please listen to my story before you do."

"All right," sighed the rider. "But you will have to be quick. I have important business to attend to."

When Mahan had finished telling his story, the rider said, "It is true there is no power but God and no strength but in God, for you, my friend, have survived not only one demon, but three. The man and wife were clever ghouls, known as Hayla and Dayla. They usually drag their victims into a pit and chop them to pieces. They work by night and only stop at daybreak. The moment the sun rises, they flee. Give thanks to God, my friend, for you have escaped death, not once, but twice! If you want," the rider continued, "I can lend you my spare mount. But you must promise to ride without saying a word."

Mahan gave his promise all too eagerly and they rode away as fast as the wind, through mountains and plains, until they reached a land as flat as the palm of your hand.

At first, Mahan could see nothing, then he heard the sound of a hundred lutes playing and voices saying, "Come this way! Come and drink some wine with us!"

Looking closer, he saw, instead of grass and flowers, thousands of demons and ghouls squatting in the dust like long black leeches, jumping up and down and ripping up the plants around them. They clapped and danced and made such a racket that their voices echoed like a hundred cymbals.

Suddenly Mahan saw from afar a thousand torches carried by creatures more terrifying than anything in a bad dream. They wore hats of tar and cloaks of pitch. Their heads were half elephant, half ox, for they had horns and tusks. Their lips were enormous and flames lashed out of their mouths instead of tongues. It seemed to Mahan that the whole world was dancing to the sound of their drums.

The moment Mahan's horse heard the noise the ghouls were making, he started to prance wildly, lifting his hooves as for a dance. Mahan looked down and saw, to his horror, that he was no longer seated on a horse, but a seven-headed dragon with scaly wings!

"What's happening?" he cried out in terror for, without further ado, the dragon started to join the dance and he had to clasp his arms and legs tightly around its long neck in order not to fall off.

Not only did the dragon dance, but it also twisted, writhed, wriggled and squirmed like a serpent gone mad. Poor Mahan was tossed around, right and left, up and down. The mad caper continued all night. Mahan was exhausted and terrified. Fearing he would fall and be trampled, he held onto the dragon with all his might.

When dawn came at last with its golden light, the dragon suddenly stopped dancing, threw Mahan to the ground and sped away, far from the dancing crowd.

As the first rays of sun touched the desert, the dancing demons also stopped and fled, and Mahan found himself alone once again, dumped on the sand like a sack of potatoes. He lay there for a long time as if dead. His head was throbbing from tiredness. He was sweating and covered in bruises, and quite unable to stir himself.

When Mahan finally opened his eyes, all he could see was a huge carpet of sand stretching before him for mile upon mile.

"Not more desert!" he sighed. "I have had enough of this gritty white stuff." So he stood up, stretched his aching legs and started running nonstop, pausing only at the first sign of greenery. A field lay before him, and a babbling stream, shining in the evening light.

He stopped, tasted the sparkling water and washed himself thoroughly. His tired heart felt young again.

"What a wonderful place to rest my tired feet and weary self!" thought Mahan. "I must find somewhere safe to sleep the night."

He looked around carefully and thanked providence when he found a small cave, the floor covered with dead leaves that formed a soft mattress. He tumbled in and snuggled down comfortably, like a bird in its nest.

He was woken by a light shining in his face. The ray of light was as narrow as a coin on its side, but bright enough to light up the small cave. Mahan stood up, searching around for the source of the light. He quickly found that it was simply moonlight streaming in through a small hole at the back of the cave. Digging at the soft earth with his hands, Mahan widened the gap until his head could pass through.

Lo and behold, there before him, stretching into the distance, was one of the most beautiful gardens he had ever seen! He dug furiously away at the hole to widen it further, so that his shoulders and body could wriggle through.

When he was finally standing on the other side of the cave, he felt he was in paradise! Dozens of cypress trees grew there, mingled with box, palms, apple and pear trees. The apples shone like carnelian and the pears glowed like amber. The pomegranates were bursting with ripeness like boxes full of treasure, and the pistachios made his lips quiver with delight. Rows of juicy peaches hung from their branches like great ruby necklaces, and the aroma of bananas was as sweet as honey from a hive. Dates and figs glowed like garnets, and fresh green almonds shone like emeralds. Purple grapes hung in dusky clusters on the vine, and oranges and lemons glittered like small lanterns in the moonlight.

Mahan forgot all about his troubles and walked around tasting the luscious fruits. He was so hungry and so glad to be in a peaceful place at last that he ate very fast, smacking his lips with pleasure and licking the juice off them. Not the proper thing to do in heaven!

Suddenly he heard a voice shouting, "Stop, thief! Stop this minute, I say!"

An old man appeared from nowhere, waving a club with one hand and raging, "Who are you? What brings you here? How dare you come into my garden without permission and steal my fruit?"

"My name is Mahan," the trembling youth replied. "I am a stranger, far from home. I have lost my way and am looking for a place to rest my weary soul."

Hearing Mahan's excuse and remembering his duties toward lost strangers, the old man grew calmer and kinder. He threw aside his club and asked Mahan to sit beside him and tell his story.

When Mahan had finished, the old man said, "You must give thanks to God, my child, for you have escaped the clutches of death, not once, but thrice!"

"What is the place that I have escaped from?" Mahan asked.

"The country that surrounds my garden is demon land, my child. It is as bare as a desert and as hot as a mine. The demons that live there pretend they are humans. They pounce on travelers and lead them astray, then torture them. They speak to you so sweetly that you follow them willingly. You think they care but in fact they don't. All they want is for you to be dead."

"Then I must rejoice," said Mahan, "for tonight I am reborn!"

61

"You are indeed, my son, for your heart is a simple and trusting one. Demons like the ones you have met pounce only on those whose souls are weak. If you are strong at heart, no demon can sway you to his side."

"Your words are wise and true, old man," said Mahan with a sigh.

"Let us forget the past and think of the future," the old man said. "I own this garden and a palace as well. My caskets are full of gold and precious jewels. My stalls are busy and my customers happy. The only thing I do not have is a child to inherit my wealth. I would like to make you my son."

Giving Mahan no time to answer, the old man continued, "If you agree, I will put all I have in your name. I will even find you a bride. All I need is time to prepare your wedding."

Mahan could not believe his luck. "Could such happiness follow such torment?" he asked himself. He stood up at once and kissed the old man's hand, saying, "I promise to obey all your commands."

"Very well then," said the old man. "Follow me. I will show you where you will spend the night. But beware of the Evil Eye; it will lead you astray if you let down your guard even for a moment."

"I will be careful from now on," Mahan promised. "I am so tired of adventures."

"This is where you will spend the night," said the old man, showing Mahan a small hut built in a sandalwood tree. "It is a safe place, with food and drink and a bed to sleep on. You must wait for me patiently and not come down from this tree. You must not talk to anyone, no matter what they ask or want."

The old man then showed Mahan a ladder made of leather and said, "Climb into the hut and pull the ladder up after you. Do not let anyone trick you into coming back down again. Stay put until I return tomorrow and make you my son and heir."

With these words, the old man set off for his palace. Mahan climbed the ladder, pulled it up after him, and settled in the tree house, ready for a quiet night. He ate some bread and drank some water and sat down on the bed, admiring the carpet under his feet.

He was barely there a moment before he heard shuffling noises and giggling, and the window of the hut was filled with a flickering light. Looking down, he saw seventeen candles held aloft by seventeen brides. Each wore a different dress and each looked like a princess. Under the tree where he was hiding they spread a carpet and silk cushions worthy of a king and queen.

A moment later, their queen arrived. She sat in the middle and they arranged themselves around her, playing music and singing the most beautiful songs. The music was so lovely that even the birds that had gone to bed woke up and listened to the concert.

Then some of the maidens stood up and danced, beating their feet and swaying their bodies elegantly, like reeds bending in the current.

Mahan could barely control himself. He wanted to go down and join the dance. But he remembered what the old man had said about weak-minded people falling prey to demons. So he stayed in the tree, not taking any chances.

When the dance had finished, food was brought, served on golden trays scattered with rubies and pearls. The dishes smelled delicious, of musk and rosewater, cinnamon and saffron.

There was pomegranate soup sweetened with sugar, followed by roast lamb, grilled fish, guinea fowl and flat bread that melted in the mouth. For dessert there were many kinds of cakes covered in nuts and syrup, which tasted delicious.

While they were eating, the queen of the maidens said to her chief attendant, "My lady, can you smell a human hiding in the sandalwood tree? I am sure that he would love some company! Just go and ask him if he would like to share our feast. Please tell him to hurry, for one should not keep ladies waiting!"

So the maiden went to the tree where Mahan was hiding and invited him to the feast in a voice as sweet as a nightingale's. She herself was as pretty as a rosebud, and poor Mahan totally forgot the advice of the old man. Down the tree he went, straight to the queen, who bade him sit on the carpet and served him wine and food with her own hands. Mahan was in seventh heaven: he was eating the most delicious dishes in the company of the most beautiful women and listening to the most exquisite music!

The queen, with whom he had fallen in love at once, had cheeks as red as apples, skin as white as milk and hair as black as night. He wanted so much to kiss her lips. "I'll bet they taste like red cherries," he thought, "or maybe strawberries."

Just as he was putting his arms around her shoulders, and closing his eyes to kiss her, the queen turned into an afreet — a horrible demon, worse than any he had met so far. Her jaws were as wide as a cavern, her back hunched like a rock. Her nose was as hot as an oven and her mouth as deep as a soup tureen.

She took hold of Mahan and smothered him with kisses. Her arms ended in hooves instead of hands and her breath smelled of dead fish.

When Mahan saw this horrible sight, he screamed like a newborn child and begged her to let him go.

"Why on earth should I do that?" was the demon's answer. "You liked me well enough before!"

So she continued kissing the poor man all night long until he fainted from exhaustion and fright. When the sun rose from behind the clouds, Mahan woke up and saw, instead of the beautiful garden, a scene of desolation. The flowers were blackened weeds, the trees had become thorn bushes, the fruits were rotten and ant-ridden, the birds had turned into snakes and the musical instruments were heaps of bones. The leftovers of the delicious feast stank like trash left outside for a week.

Mahan was brokenhearted once again. The old man would never make him his heir now. He cried his heart out until there were no tears left. Then he turned to the only friend he had left: God. He knelt down, touching his face to the ground, and prayed for forgiveness and guidance.

Mahan stayed there for quite a long time, asking himself questions like: "What shall I do now, and what does it all mean?"

Suddenly he felt a hand on his shoulder. Turning around, he beheld the most beautiful person he had ever seen: a being of light, with a face as radiant as a star and clothes as green as new leaves in spring.

"Who are you, my lord?" Mahan asked in wonder.

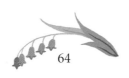

"My name is Khidr," smiled the being of light. "I am sent by Him to whom you have just prayed. I have come to take you home. Just give me your hand and close your eyes. All will soon be well."

Mahan could not believe his luck. He quickly took the stranger's hand, closed his eyes and prayed a little longer. When he opened them again, Khidr had disappeared. He looked around and saw that he was back under the palm trees, by the Nile, where his adventures had begun.

"How long did my adventures last?" he asked himself. "For days, or years even?"

He did not want to think about it any more, so he rushed back to the house where the party had been held and saw his friends gathered there. They were dressed all in blue for mourning, but still praying for his safe return.

"How lucky I am to have such good friends!" said Mahan, moved by their loyalty. "I missed you more than you will ever guess," he told them as he embraced each in turn. "I am so happy to be in your midst once more. You have no idea what lies beyond this town," the young man continued. "There are demons out there, waiting to pounce on those who have weak minds. Thank you for waiting for me, my friends. From now on I shall wear only blue robes," Mahan declared. "For blue is the color of the sky, to which we will all return one day. It is the color of the sea and of infinity, and it reminds me of Him who created me, and to whom I owe infinite thanks."

"Blue is the color of forget-me-nots, of bluebells, blueberries and lapis lazuli," said Princess Azaryun, finishing her story.

"Blue is the color of peace and calm," answered the shah. "It is the color of your eyes, my dear princess, and of the sapphires around your neck and the turquoises on your dress."

"Blue is also my favorite color," Azaryun said, "which is why I dress all in blue and why I made the Blue Pavilion my home."

The Story of Good and Bad

Told on Thursday by the Chinese Princess

One Thursday morning, Bahram woke up with the smell of sandalwood and musk filling the air. He remembered that it was the day for visiting the Chinese princess in the Sandalwood Pavilion of Jupiter.

"Bring me my brown robe and my brown turban with the tiger-eye clasp," he called to his servants. Then he jumped out of bed and started to prepare himself for his visit.

The princess's name was Yaghma-Naz. She had straight black hair and eyes the color of chestnuts. Her lips were like fresh dates, her skin like porcelain. She moved with grace, sang like a nightingale, and could paint on silk lustrous landscapes, butterflies and flowers.

After admiring her paintings and listening to some enchanting music, Bahram shared a Chinese meal with the princess. Noodles with bean sprouts were served, along with bamboo shoots and water chestnuts, followed by honeyed chicken and lychees in syrup.

"Will you tell me why you chose to live in the Sandalwood Pavilion, and why you love brown, the color of sandalwood?" asked Shah Bahram. "I am eager to hear your story."

So, while Bahram sipped jasmine tea, Yaghma-Naz began her tale.

Two young men decided to go on a long journey through the desert to another town. They were as different as day and night. One was called Kheyr, for he was gentle and kind. The other was called Sharr, for he was nasty and wicked. Their names mirrored their natures for in Arabic, Kheyr means "good" and Sharr means "bad."

Both carried provisions on their back and waterskins in their bags. The journey was long and the desert was hot, and Kheyr had soon drunk all his water.

"I am sure there will be water further on," he told himself.

Sharr, who knew better, had kept aside one waterskin, hidden at the bottom of his bag. Being a wicked man, he did not mention this to Kheyr.

Kheyr was getting thirsty and weak. Whenever they stopped for a nap, Sharr would drink secretly from his remaining waterskin while his companion slept.

Kheyr continued walking without complaint. His throat was dry and his head was burning. At last he fell onto the sand, unable to move any further, and said, "I need water, my friend. I cannot bear it any longer."

Sharr laughed at him and said, "How stupid can you get? How can you go through the desert hoping to find water? There isn't an oasis around every corner!" With these words, Sharr drew his waterskin from his bag and drank openly in front of his friend, without sharing a drop.

Kheyr looked at him with sad eyes and a sadder heart. "How can you be a friend when you refuse to share your water? How can you lie to me and see me in despair?"

"Who said we are friends?" Sharr answered. "Each man for himself, says the law of the jungle!"

"This is not a jungle and we are not animals," Kheyr replied. "In the name of friendship, I ask you for just a drop, for my thirst is killing me."

"Then die!" said Sharr, teasing Kheyr by drinking some more.

"Look, friend," said Kheyr. "Deep in the pocket of my bag are two rubies as big as cherries. Take them and give me water in exchange."

"I know your tricks," Sharr answered. "You give me the rubies now but, when we reach the town, you will tell people I have stolen them from you. No thanks, I don't want your rubies."

"What do you want, then?" Kheyr asked.

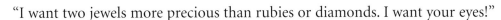

"I want two jewels more precious than rubies or diamonds. I want your eyes!"

"My eyes in exchange for water? You must be joking, my friend!"

"Not at all," Sharr answered. "If you want water, that is the deal."

Kheyr spent the night in agony, thinking of ways to solve his problem. When morning came, he was so desperate for a drink that he told himself, "If I die of thirst, what use are my eyes? I would prefer to be blind than to die."

He then called his so-called friend, saying, "Wake up! Bring your dagger and take my eyes in exchange for water! It seems that your heart has become as hard as ice."

Sharr, who was waiting for this moment all night, drew out his dagger and took Kheyr's eyes out. He then drank the water himself, spat on his friend and went off laughing, taking with him the two rubies and all Kheyr's money.

Kheyr could not believe his eyes that Sharr could be so wicked. But what eyes should he believe, for he had none left! So he rolled on the ground, rubbing his forehead in the dust, moaning loudly and losing blood.

Not far from where Kheyr lay, almost dead, was a Kurdish camp of seven to eight tents. Their chief was good, noble and fair. He brought his flock there every year for pasture. The Kurdish chief had a daughter, with dark hair that fell in waves well below her shoulders. Her eyes were the color of violets and her lips were as red as pomegranates. She had a small mole on her cheek and her face shone like the full moon.

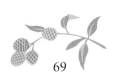

She came that morning to the spring that lay nearby to draw some water to drink. Hearing soft moans a little way off, she rushed to see who it was. It was Kheyr, of course! If he had eyes to see himself, he would have died of fright for he looked almost dead. But the chief's daughter, who had a good and loving heart, bent over and turned him around. She saw his face covered in blood and a pair of eyes lying beside him in the dust.

"What happened to you, poor man?" she asked. "Who is the monster who did this to you?"

In a voice as faint as a baby's breath, Kheyr said, "Please give me some water, I beg of you!"

The chief's daughter, who had a jar full of water, lifted Kheyr's head and poured a few drops into his mouth. She then washed his face and his wounds and gave him some more to drink. This time he could not stop drinking. His dried-up soul felt alive once more, as if the Water of Life was pouring into him. And for the first time since his misfortunes began, his face broke into a crooked smile.

After a little while, Kheyr had enough strength in him to tell his story to the chief's daughter. When he had finished, she immediately picked up the bleeding eyes and put them gently back into their sockets, binding them with a bandage around his head. "Come with me to my father's camp," she said. "He will help you get well."

She then helped Kheyr get back on his feet and, holding him by the hand, guided him to the camp. Back at her father's tent, she asked a servant to prepare a bed for him and give him meat broth and bread to eat.

Kheyr, who was starving, ate his fill, then settled for a long rest. When sunset came, the Kurdish chief returned to find a guest sleeping in his tent.

"Where does this man come from?" he asked his daughter. "What happened to his eyes?"

She explained everything, then said, "Father, you know a lot about herbs and potions and spells. Do you know a way to make this man see again?"

The chief thought for a while and said, "There is a tree beside the spring where you went this morning. It is about thirty feet tall. Its leaves look like leather and it smells like a flower. It is a sandalwood tree. Its roots are used for oils, while its wood is made into precious boxes. Go to that tree and get me some of its leaves. Crush them well, then

strain the juice and put it straight onto this man's eyes. It will take away the pain and help him recover his sight."

The daughter did as she was told and poured the sandalwood juice onto Kheyr's wounds. For five days in a row she did this, bandaging the eyes with clean pads and making him sleep and rest and forget the evil that had befallen him.

On the sixth day, Kheyr woke up feeling much better. The chief's daughter came to him with breakfast and removed the bandage to see the effect of her medicine. Kheyr looked at her with perfectly healthy eyes, which beheld her beauty for the first time. No words could express the happiness and gratitude that Kheyr felt. Not only was he happy to have his eyes back, but he fell in love at once with the maiden who had restored his sight. Wanting to show how grateful he was, he went straight to her father to ask if he could help in any way. The Kurdish chief asked him to guard his flock, keeping his camels and sheep away from wolves and thieves. Kheyr did it so well, expecting no payment, that the chief said to him one day, "What present would you like, my son, for all that you have done for us?"

"There is a very precious jewel that you possess. She has violet eyes and long dark locks. She helped me find my eyes again. Without her my life would be worthless."

The Kurdish chief understood at once Kheyr's request, and went to ask his daughter if she agreed.

"Of course, Father," was her reply. "Can't you see that Kheyr and I were made for each other? We promise to give you many grandchildren to be your heirs!"

The Kurdish chief ordered a wedding feast to be held for seven days and seven nights. All the neighboring tribes were invited. They came with precious gifts and rare spices. They danced all day and all night, in sunlight and in firelight, until there were no more songs to dance to, no more feet to dance with and no more food to eat.

The Kurdish chief gave the bride and groom a big bag of gold, some precious carpets and enough camels and sheep to make them rich for the rest of their lives. He then blessed them and wished them luck. There were many cries and sighs when the young couple left, for Kheyr was taking his bride back home, as was the Kurdish custom.

On their way out of the camp, Kheyr and his bride passed the sandalwood tree that had saved his sight. He took two bagfuls of leaves and asked his wife not to tell anyone about them.

After several days of travel, they reached a town where everyone was walking around crying and wringing their hands.

"What is the matter, dear friends?" Kheyr asked.

"Our king's daughter has terrible fits. She shakes then collapses, lifeless and exhausted. Our king is so sad that he has forgotten how to rule. He spends all his days by his daughter's bed asking for one doctor after another. Many doctors have come and gone, offering this cure and that. But none have succeeded in helping the poor princess."

"I believe I can help her," Kheyr said.

"Be careful, young man," the people answered. "Many doctors have lost their heads because they failed to cure her. The king has now declared that whoever cures his daughter will have her hand in marriage."

"Go tell your king," Kheyr said, "that there is a man in town who can cure his daughter, not for a crown or a kingdom but for the love of God."

The people were truly astonished.

"Who is this man?" they whispered.

Kheyr's reputation reached the chief with the speed of flames through dry tinder. He immediately asked to see him.

"What is your name, good man?" the chief asked. "And what can you do for my daughter?"

"My name is Kheyr, which means 'good,' and I believe I have the perfect medicine for your daughter."

"I hope your medicine is like your name. Go now to my daughter's room and see what you can do. You know the rule: if she is not better, your head goes on top of that ladder for all to see. If you can cure her, though, her hand is yours."

Kheyr went to the princess's room and looked upon her face as beautiful as the moon, twitching with pain. Her body was trembling and she was moaning softly.

He took out one bagful of sandalwood leaves and ground them into a fine powder that he mixed with fresh water. He asked the maid to give it to the princess then leave her to rest.

For three days the princess drank and slept. On the third day, she raised her head and said, "Bring me some food. I am starving."

The king could not believe his ears. His daughter was finally eating! He rushed to her bedside and saw her finishing a big plate of rice, lamb and nuts. No sign of trembling, twitching, or moaning.

"How is my darling today?" the king asked.

"As happy as a lark!" the princess answered. "Who is this doctor who found a cure for my fits?"

"He is a young man called Kheyr, who came from nowhere carrying a bag. He gave you something to drink and in three days you woke up and said, 'Give me food. I am starving!'"

The princess laughed like a dozen tinkling bells. The king was so pleased to see his daughter happy and healthy again that he sent for Kheyr and told him, "You kept your word; I will keep mine. I know you desired no reward for curing my daughter, but I said I would give you her hand in marriage, and I will do so. I have just ordered the carriage that will take you to the wedding hall. May God bless you, my son, for you are truly a lucky one. Not only will you be marrying my only daughter but, when I die, you will take over from me."

Kheyr accepted with gratitude. He loved both his wives equally and they all lived happily. The two women did everything together, just like twin sisters. The townspeople were happy, too, for their king was finally free to take care of them. They put up banners that read "Long live the king and his new heir. May God give them wisdom to rule this kingdom well."

But our story does not end yet, for we have yet to see what happened to Sharr. As for the second bag of sandalwood leaves, it was still waiting to be used.

Indeed, the occasion soon arose. The king had a powerful minister, a vizier who advised him on all matters. The vizier also had a lovely daughter who had smallpox when she was two. The illness had left her blind. Her father had searched far and wide for a doctor who would restore his daughter's sight.

When he heard of the princess's miraculous recovery, he asked for Kheyr to come and examine his daughter's eyes.

"I think I have a cure for them, my lord," was Kheyr's reply. "Just leave me with your daughter for a while."

Kheyr took his second bag of sandalwood leaves, crushed them into a powder and added enough water to form a paste. He put it on the eyes of the vizier's daughter and bandaged them up. He then asked her to lie in bed for three days and three nights. Afterward, he said, she would see the beauty of the sunset.

And so it was. On the third day the lovely maiden rose and watched the sun go down in shades of pink, red and orange. She was as happy as a child who suddenly realizes she can read and write.

"Bring me the person who saved my sight," the maiden cried, "for without him I would still be blind. I must thank him for his good deed. He has saved me from a life of darkness and brought me back my happiness."

When the maiden saw Kheyr dressed in his princely robes and looking as handsome as a tree in bloom, she fell in love with him and asked her father if she could marry him.

"The law says you can marry up to four women, as long as you treat them equally," the vizier said to Kheyr. "Can your heart embrace all three and can you divide your time between them equally?"

"I believe I can, my lord," was Kheyr's answer.

So all three wives lived happily together in a palace next to the king's. When the king died, Kheyr took his place on the throne. He ruled with wisdom, justice and kindness, and was loved by all.

One morning, Kheyr, who was looking from the palace window, saw two men arguing.

With a start, he recognized one of them as being his former friend, Sharr. He asked one of his servants to call him into the palace courtyard.

Sharr, who was terrified of being summoned by the king's man, stood in the courtyard trembling. When Kheyr arrived, Sharr did not recognize him. He bent down and kissed the king's hand, asking his forgiveness for having disturbed him.

"What is your name?" Kheyr asked.

"My name is Mubashir," Sharr lied. "I travel from town to town selling my goods and bringing good news."

"Tell me your real name," Kheyr asked. "Lying to the king is not advisable."

"I have no other name," Sharr lied again.

"You are a liar and a thief," Kheyr said, "and a heartless friend too. Don't you recognize who stands here before you? I am the man whose eyes you took out and whom you left in the desert to die of thirst. You stole my rubies and all my gold and went away laughing at my pain. Your name is 'Bad' just like your acts. But God is just and fair. Here we meet again, me a king and you a simple traveler."

Sharr could not believe his eyes that it was Kheyr standing there wearing a crown and ordering him around. He fell to the floor and kissed his feet, begging for forgiveness.

"Have mercy on me, great king. Forgive me for having hurt you, but my name is Bad and my actions are too, while your name is Good and you are too."

Kheyr, who did not have an ounce of wickedness in him but was full of forgiveness, ordered his guards to take Sharr outside the city gates and banned him from ever coming back in again.

Outside the gates was the desert, where the Kurdish chief happened to be passing by with his huntsmen. Seeing the king's guards throw a man out, he went to them and asked, "What did this man do to deserve such treatment?"

"He has stolen from our king," the guards answered.

"Empty your pockets, now!" the Kurdish chief ordered Sharr.

When the wretched man had emptied them, can you guess what fell to the ground? The two rubies, of course! Sharr had never sold them, for he thought they were his lucky stones. At this moment they were not, for the Kurdish chief remembered the story that Kheyr had told him about the man who had robbed him, taken out his eyes and left him for dead.

The Kurdish chief was a fair man, but a hard one too. Outside the city gates was his domain. He ordered Sharr to be killed on the spot and went to the palace to give Kheyr back his rubies.

"You gave me back my jewels long ago," Kheyr replied. "You gave me back my eyes and entrusted me with your precious daughter. These rubies are yours now, stepfather."

He was sad that Sharr had been killed, and prayed for his soul to find peace. Kheyr was known in all the desert towns as the fairest of kings and the wisest of all. When he needed time to be by himself, to think about a problem and how to resolve it best, he would go to the sandalwood tree whose leaves had restored his sight and given him his three wives. He used to sit in its shade and pray, asking God for guidance and thanking him for granting him a kingdom.

Kheyr loved that tree so much that he wore only robes the color of sandal-wood. He ordered his court to wear the same, saying, "Sandalwood makes the soul at peace. It has a lovely smell and puts people at ease. Sandalwood can cure headaches and fevers. It heals wounds and is good for the liver. The earth is the color of sandalwood and everything that comes from the earth is good."

"What a lovely story that was," Shah Bahram said. "Now I understand your love of sandalwood, dear Yaghma-Naz. When fall comes, I must plant many sandalwood trees in the palace gardens."

"What a wonderful idea!" was Yaghma-Naz's reply.

The Unfortunate Lovers

Told on Friday by the Persian Princess

One Friday morning Shah Bahram woke up to a sky full of fluffy white clouds. He looked out of the window and smiled.

"Quick, bring me my white silk robe," he told his servants, "and my white hat with the diamond as big as a plum. Today I am going to visit the Persian princess."

The dome of the White Pavilion was covered with mother-of-pearl. Its walls were made of white marble and its windows of the clearest crystal. The garden was filled with white flowers. The almond and cherry trees were in full blossom. Daisies smiled in the grass and lotus flowers offered their petals to the sky. Their sweet fragrance floated on the spring air.

"Welcome to the White Pavilion of Venus, Majesty," said Princess Durr-Siti. She was wearing a white dress embroidered with pearls and a garland of daisies around her blonde hair. The scent of jasmine floated around her and a white Persian cat stood purring by her feet.

"Would Your Majesty care for some orange-blossom tea?" asked the princess. "Served with rice pudding and pine nuts?"

They sat on white cushions as they ate from silver bowls, drank tea from crystal cups, and listened to the most haunting love songs. The singer was, of course, dressed in snowy white and played a very old silver harp.

"These songs are beautiful," said the shah. "What about a story to go with them? Can you tell me why you chose to live in the White Pavilion, and why the color white is so special to you?"

"I can, Your Majesty! Let me tell you a story while we walk in the garden."

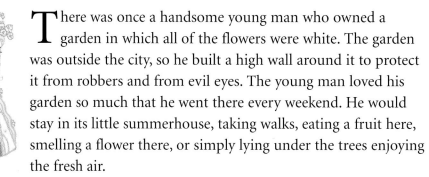

There was once a handsome young man who owned a garden in which all of the flowers were white. The garden was outside the city, so he built a high wall around it to protect it from robbers and from evil eyes. The young man loved his garden so much that he went there every weekend. He would stay in its little summerhouse, taking walks, eating a fruit here, smelling a flower there, or simply lying under the trees enjoying the fresh air.

One Friday, he was so eager to see his beloved garden that he skipped the midday prayers and rushed to the countryside. To his dismay, he found the garden locked like a box. In his haste he had forgotten to bring the key, and the gardener was nowhere to be seen.

He banged on the gate and shouted for someone to open it, but no one was there to hear or to care. Tired and desperate, the young man sat sweating in the heat of the midday sun, waiting by the gate for the gardener to return. He dozed off a little, then, to his surprise, he was woken by the sound of lutes and harps and sweet love songs. Through a hole in the gate he saw to his astonishment a dozen maidens, all dressed in white. The maidens were dancing around the fruit trees, whose branches were waving to the rhythm of the music.

"How can one watch such a party and just sit here like a stone?" the young man asked himself. "I must find a way into my garden, I must!" he muttered.

So off he went around his high garden wall, looking for an opening or a hole until he found one, as small as a fist, by the gate itself. It took him some time to make it bigger, but he slid through the gap like a clever snake and fell right in front of two maidens who were guarding the gate.

"Stop there, thief!" they shouted. "How dare you come into a private property? You deserve a good thrashing!"

"I am not a thief!" the young man replied indignantly. "I am the owner of this garden, and I could ask what you are doing here yourselves!"

"How come you don't have a key?" the girls replied, ignoring his last remark. "You are either a thief or a spy and we don't believe a word you're saying!"

The argument lasted for a while, then the girls decided to believe him for he looked handsome and pleasant, and, besides, they were tired of guarding the gate and wanted to go back and join the fun.

"Come with us," they said. "We'll take you to a hiding place where you can

80

watch the dancers. If you like one of them, we shall bring her to you and you can spend an hour or two together."

So saying, they took him into the summerhouse to a balcony from which he could watch everything through a chink in the floor.

Directly below him was a white marble fountain filled with the purest water and shining with silvery fish. Around it grew lilies, narcissi and jasmine, and in it some maidens were dipping their feet. Their skin was as white as pearl, for some had removed their veils while others had removed all. They played with the fish and sang songs, laughing and chatting happily.

"Which one shall I choose?" the young man asked himself. "They all look so beautiful and so charming."

Then he noticed the harpist, who was as fair as the morning sun, with lips as dark as ripe dates. She played such lovely tunes that whoever heard her was bewitched. Compared to her dazzling beauty, the others were as pale as moons.

At this moment, the two maidens came back and asked, "Whom have you decided to choose?"

"The fair harpist, of course," the young man answered.

"We shall bring her to you," was their reply.

As he waited, the young man grew worried that the harpist would refuse to come, for she was worthy of a shah. Luckily for him, the maidens returned holding her by the hand, and introduced them to each other.

"What is your name?" the young man asked.

"Bakht," she said, lowering her eyes.

"Does it mean good fortune?" he inquired.

"Indeed it does, sir," was her reply.

"Then knowing you will bring me luck," he declared.

"A thousand times, I hope," she concluded.

The maidens slipped quietly from the balcony, giving them a chance to get to know each other in peace.

For an hour they talked of this and that. Then the young man decided it was time for a kiss, so he came gently closer to Bakht and looked deep into her eyes. He held her face in his hands and was about to touch her lips, when the balcony suddenly collapsed beneath them and, with a frightful crash, they fell onto the grass below, right in front of the dancing maidens.

Imagine how they felt! Embarrassed, of course, and wanting to hide their heads in shame. But at least they were unhurt.

Bakht quickly sat down with her friends, pretending nothing was the matter. She went back to her harp and started playing a new tune while the young man hurried out of sight and hid behind a bush, with tears in his eyes. He listened to her song:

> *"How long must I hide my love for you?*
> *True love has no regrets, nor fears*
> *When sharp swords bar its way.*
> *True lovers will never feel*
> *Tired, defeated or dismayed."*

Feeling sorry for her, the two maidens came once again to the young man. "Be patient," they said, "and wait for nighttime. We shall send Bakht to you then."

When night covered the garden with its dark velvet cloth, the young man led Bakht to his favorite cypress tree. Under its branches they sat together, like lovebirds of a similar feather. He looked at her with loving eyes and touched her hair that shone like sand in the sun. He brought his lips closer to hers and was about to kiss her when a wild cat, crouching on a branch above them, about to pounce on a bird, suddenly missed its footing and fell on them.

They both sprang up like two jack-in-a-boxes and ran as fast as their feet could carry them. Their hearts were pounding very fast and they both had tears in their eyes. It was the second time they had been disturbed. Once again, they were upset, but not hurt.

The lovely Bakht went back to her friends, took up her harp and sang softly in a sad voice:

> *"There was a shah who had a rose*
> *He used to visit every day.*
> *A nightingale perched among her branches,*
> *Singing a lovely lullaby to her.*
> *There was a cat that saw the bird*
> *And pounced on its throat.*
> *The poor shah looked at the rose;*
> *Her petals had fallen off in shock."*

Bakht's friends listened to the song and understood how difficult things had been for her and for the handsome youth. They decided to help them once again.

They took them to the biggest tree in the garden whose spreading branches formed little seats. The lovers chose the highest branch they could climb to and settled on it, holding hands and gazing into each other's eyes. They were just about to kiss, when a field mouse that was hiding in the tree, waiting to pounce on some lovely ripe gourds, cut the gourds' stems with one bite, causing them to crash to the ground.

The lovers were terrified by the noise. They thought the cook had come after them from the summerhouse, clattering his pots and pans. Jumping down from the tree, they ran off in different directions, leaving their shoes behind them. Bakht went back to her friends and the young man lay down in a corner of the garden, exhausted and upset. Closing his eyes for a rest, he heard Bakht sing:

> *"Once upon a time there were two lovers*
> *Who wanted so much to see each other*
> *They tried to meet night and day*
> *But ended up going their own way.*
> *Once it was a mouse, another time a cat*
> *Who pounced on them as if upon a rat.*
> *Young lovers should always take care*
> *When arranging to meet. They must beware."*

Again, Bakht's friends decided to help, for they felt pity for her. So they went again in search of the handsome youth. They found him lying in the moonlight with tears glistening on his cheek like dewdrops.

"What is wrong with you both?" they asked. "Why can't you find a quiet place where no one will disturb you?"

"We tried but failed," the youth replied. "But we shall try again."

Once again, Bakht met the handsome young man, this time in a cave hidden by a curtain of jasmine. The youth took Bakht inside and they sat down upon a bed of rose petals. She is the sweetest of flowers, thought the young man as he kissed her. He had barely kissed her once, when a family of foxes, which had taken refuge in the cave, caught sight of a wolf hiding there too. Like lightning they fled, one after another, the wolf in hot pursuit. Right over the two lovers they ran, scratching them and trampling on them. Trembling with fear, the young people fled to opposite ends of the garden.

"Enough is enough," Bakht's friends ordered her. "This young man cannot be good for you. Wherever he takes you, there is no peace. You must let him go."

"It is not his fault," Bakht pleaded. "Wherever we go, we are spied on by evil eyes and strange beasts."

"This must be a sign from heaven," sighed the youth, stepping out from behind the tree where he had been hiding.

"What sign is that?" Bakht's friends asked curiously.

"A sign to make her my bride," the youth declared. "You see, the collapsing balcony, the cat and mouse, the foxes and wolf were all trying to say, 'Wed her! Wed her! Wed her before you kiss her!'"

Indeed, the youth did just that. He married his lovely Bakht in the garden among the roses and the jasmine. The maidens sprinkled their path with rose petals and rice, for good luck, and danced for them until past midnight. When the wedding feast was over, the groom kissed the bride, and do you know what? Not a sound was heard, not an animal was in sight — no cats or mice, foxes or wolves came near them!

"My intuition was right," the youth thought, kissing his bride again. "We had to get married first."

They were happily married for many years. Every Friday, after the midday prayers, they came to their garden and sat beneath the tree where the mouse had spied the gourds, and remembered their adventures that first night. They often wondered whether a fox, a wolf, a mouse or a cat would come to disturb them, but nothing ever did.

"My garden too is to be enjoyed only by those whose souls are pure white," said Durr-Siti, her story ended. "Hence the flowers here are white, as is the day during the brightness of noon. The moon looks white on a cloudless night, as do the stars. White is the color brides choose to wear; it is the color of purity and the perfection of affairs. White is the color people wear when on a pilgrimage, and white is the color that heralds the beginning of things."

As she finished her story, evening fell and the sky darkened. The perfume of jasmine and lilies filled the air, and the whole room was bathed in the palest moonlight.

The Shah and the Shepherd

Shah Bahram had spent several months visiting the Seven Pavilions, and he emerged a wiser and happier man. It was now springtime and the earth smelled of musk. Green shoots poked their heads above the ground and the sun shone like a copper plate. Violets wore dresses of deep purple and lines of lotus flowers decorated the ponds like living necklaces. Lilies opened their hearts to the sun, showing their golden centers. Wild mint grew along the walls and the tamarisk trees gave off their odor of camphor. The willow trees displayed their buds for the nightingales to hop and strut among. The Persian New Year had arrived!

To celebrate this important date, Shah Bahram held a magnificent feast outside the palace gates. The royal fanfare sounded and sweetmeats were given to the crowds thronging outside the palace. Delighted to see the shah back again, people sang and danced and picnicked among the flowers.

When dusk came, fireworks went up, lighting the sky with purple, gold and silver dust. "What a lovely day!" exclaimed everyone as they happily wended their way home.

But the end of the day was not happy for the shah. He had barely put his feet up when a messenger entered the throne room in a tearing hurry.

"Your Majesty," he cried, "the father of the Chinese princess, Yaghma-Naz, has attacked our borders with his troops! The people living there are frightened and ask you to come to their aid."

"Call the Grand Vizier!" the shah ordered.

The Grand Vizier, the highest of the ministers, was a man called Rast-Rawshan. Sly and greedy, he had gradually emptied the treasury during the shah's visits to the Seven Pavilions, and had hidden all the money away. He was a cruel and evil man too. Whoever tried to tell the shah what was happening was either killed or imprisoned before they could warn him. So the people kept silent out of sheer terror. They went about their business on tiptoe in case Rast-Rawshan noticed them and took their money, their houses or even their lives.

"Your Majesty called?" asked the Grand Vizier in his oily voice.

"Yes, we need to send troops to the border. The Chinese are attacking!"

"But we do not have enough money in the treasury, Sire, and the troops will not move without pay."

"Strange!" exclaimed the shah. "The treasury was full of gold before I visited the Seven Pavilions and left it in your care."

"You know, Sire, things are not what they used to be. Everything costs a great deal of money these days," lied Rast-Rawshan, "like the feast you have just held."

"Very well," said Bahram, dismissing him. "We will discuss it in the morning."

The shah could not sleep a wink, however. He tossed and turned and did sums in his head, over and over again. He could not believe his money could have disappeared so fast. "There is something not quite right here," he concluded. "I must find out what it is."

So, at the first rays of light, the shah mounted his favorite horse and went riding in the desert. The early sunlight painted wonderful patterns on the sand, the air was crisp and the palm trees heavy with dates. Riding was excellent for thinking, Shah Bahram believed. So whenever he had a problem, he tried to solve it on horseback.

He rode for a while, churning the problem over in his head, until he noticed black smoke rising like a coil into the blue sky. He spurred his horse toward it. Getting closer, he saw a tent, some sheep grazing and an old man watching over them. Beside the tent was a tree, and, hanging upsidedown from one of the branches, was a dog, tied with a rope by its paws.

"That's strange!" thought the shah. "Why would anyone do this to an animal?"

"Hello, old man!" he called. "What have you done to your poor dog?"

"Only what he deserves!" the shepherd replied, rising to his feet and greeting the shah.

"What has he done to deserve such punishment?" Shah Bahram persisted.

"Please sit down, Sire, and share my meal with me. I will tell you a story that will curdle your blood!"

So Shah Bahram sat by the fire, sharing the shepherd's modest meal and listening intently to his story.

"Not so long ago," said the shepherd, "I was a wealthy man, with many sheep and a rich table and bed. This dog that you see up there was my flock's guardian, my trusted friend and my companion. For many years, he guarded my flock with tooth and claw from thieves and wolves. Whenever I needed to go to town, I knew my flock was safe with him in charge. And when my business kept me away overnight, he brought my sheep safely back home. For many years, it was a perfect friendship, based on care and trust and hardship shared.

"One day I decided to count the flock. To my surprise, I found there were seven sheep missing. Gone! I thought I had made a mistake, so I let the matter go. The following week I counted my flock again.

Again, seven were missing. I told no one about it but resolved to stay awake at night to catch the thief. But I must have dozed off for a short while on each occasion, for I could never catch anyone.

"Week by week, my flock became smaller, and, day by day, I became poorer. From owner of the flock, I became its shepherd. Despite all this, I still trusted my dog.

"One day I was dozing beside a stream having a wonderful dream of riches and a life of ease, when a wolf howling like a dog awoke me. I opened one eye but did not move, keeping my head bowed over my staff and pretending to snooze. I saw a wolf bitch approach from afar and call my dog. He ran to her like a long-lost friend, wagging his tail, happy to see her. They tumbled on the ground together, licking each other's ears. Tired of playing, my dog lay down and slept while she pretended to lie down too. When she was sure the coast was clear, she went to the nearest sheep, carried it off by the neck, and swiftly killed and ate it in four great gulps.

"My dog never heard a sound and never made a move. In fury, I took a rope, bound him by his paws and tied him upside down to this tree. He had betrayed my trust and deserved to be punished. What would you have done in my place?"

Shah Bahram had no words to say. He just nodded, thanked the shepherd for his hospitality, stood up and went straight back to his palace, with a face full of menace.

"This shepherd has taught me a true lesson of leadership," he muttered to himself. "I am like a shepherd and my subjects like my flock while my Grand Vizier, whom I trusted completely, has acted like a bad dog. He has frittered my money away somehow, and made my people poor and weak. He deserves to be punished forthwith!"

Back at the palace, Shah Bahram called his guards and ordered them to throw the Grand Vizier into prison.

"If the people see him put away," he reasoned, "they will find the courage to tell me what he did to them when my back was turned."

When the people heard that the Grand Vizier was in prison, they went in their dozens to meet the shah. They told him how Rast-Rawshan had ordered innocent people to be killed and imprisoned so that his evil ways would not be discovered. They told him how he had taken their houses, gardens, money, jewels and servants; how he had lied, cheated and above all conspired with the enemy, leaving the kingdom's borders weak and badly guarded.

The audience lasted until late at night. Shah Bahram retired to bed but could not close his eyes from the shame and pain of it all. He blamed himself for being blind and weak and for trusting such a wicked man.

Just as the sun was kissing the palm trees good morning, Shah Bahram ordered the Grand Vizier to be hanged like a thief and a cheat. He called the people to come and witness what happens to those who commit treachery. Then he invited the old shepherd to the palace, thanked him for his valuable lesson in guardianship, and gave him a new flock and a new dog.

From this time on, Shah Bahram reigned with even greater attention to justice and fairness. He made sure his treasury was once again filled with gold, and sent his soldiers back to the border to defend it with renewed vigor. Hearing that Bahram was fully in charge once again, the Chinese ruler changed his mind about attacking the frontier and ordered his troops to turn back. After all, his daughter Yaghma-Naz would have been sad to know that her father was planning to attack what was now her home.

Shah Bahram did not rest there. He ordered the Seven Pavilions to be turned into fire temples, for he believed that fire was like the light of heaven and had to be kept burning day and night to ensure all was right with the world. With a heavy heart, remembering the many happy days they had spent together, he sent the lovely princesses away, giving them rich presents of jewelry and clothing. He asked seven priests to take their place and keep the fires in the pavilions ablaze. Each priest was known as "athravan," which in Persian means "belonging to fire."

He himself turned to worship God, forgetting himself and turning his

mind to greater things. One day, he took his crown from his head and, placing it on the empty throne, set out with his courtiers to hunt. Leaving them to chase after deer, he hunted the wild donkeys. After a while he spotted a beautiful beast and spurred his horse toward it. It ran into a cave, pursued by the shah and his page. The page, afraid of what might be within, stopped at the entrance while Shah Bahram entered fearlessly. For a whole hour the page waited for his master, but when there was still no sign of him, he sounded the alarm so loudly that it must have reached heaven!

The shah's courtiers came and searched every blade of grass. They turned over every stone and looked into every hole. Still there was no sign of Bahram. With tears in their eyes, they went back to the palace and told everyone what had happened.

The whole kingdom mourned and wept for the loss of a great shah who had ruled wisely and well. For forty days and forty nights, the city was draped with black cloth as a sign of mourning. All the citizens were filled with sadness and pity for themselves and for their children. For they knew that not many shahs would be remembered as Shah Bahram would, for many centuries to come.

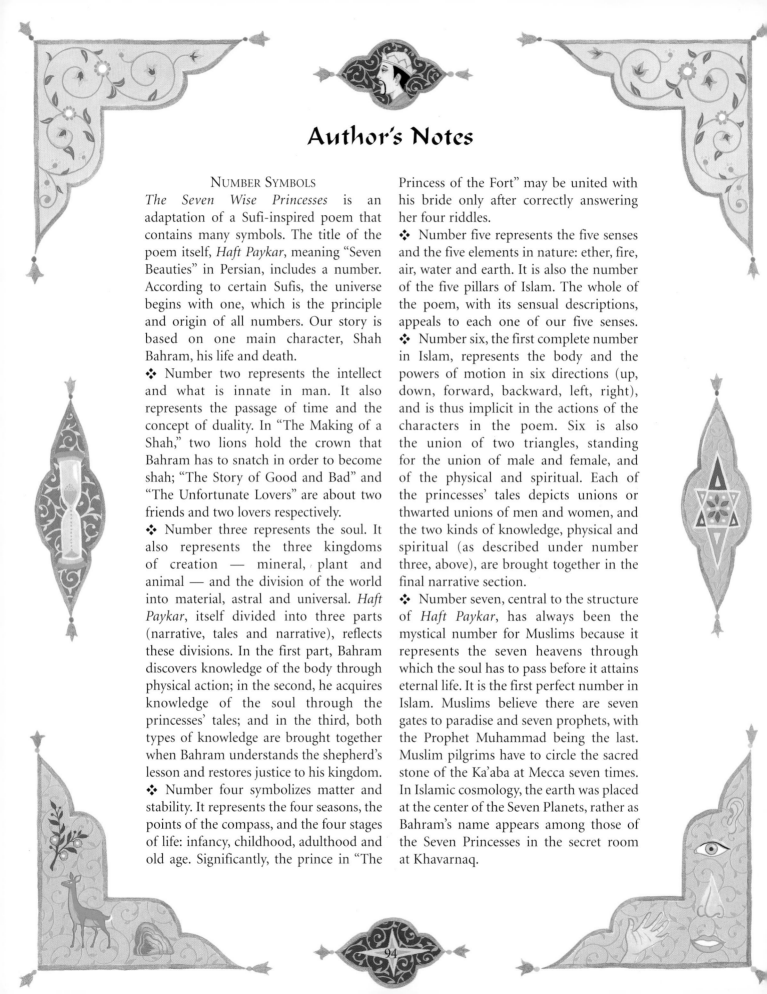

Author's Notes

NUMBER SYMBOLS

The Seven Wise Princesses is an adaptation of a Sufi-inspired poem that contains many symbols. The title of the poem itself, *Haft Paykar*, meaning "Seven Beauties" in Persian, includes a number. According to certain Sufis, the universe begins with one, which is the principle and origin of all numbers. Our story is based on one main character, Shah Bahram, his life and death.

❖ Number two represents the intellect and what is innate in man. It also represents the passage of time and the concept of duality. In "The Making of a Shah," two lions hold the crown that Bahram has to snatch in order to become shah; "The Story of Good and Bad" and "The Unfortunate Lovers" are about two friends and two lovers respectively.

❖ Number three represents the soul. It also represents the three kingdoms of creation — mineral, plant and animal — and the division of the world into material, astral and universal. *Haft Paykar*, itself divided into three parts (narrative, tales and narrative), reflects these divisions. In the first part, Bahram discovers knowledge of the body through physical action; in the second, he acquires knowledge of the soul through the princesses' tales; and in the third, both types of knowledge are brought together when Bahram understands the shepherd's lesson and restores justice to his kingdom.

❖ Number four symbolizes matter and stability. It represents the four seasons, the points of the compass, and the four stages of life: infancy, childhood, adulthood and old age. Significantly, the prince in "The Princess of the Fort" may be united with his bride only after correctly answering her four riddles.

❖ Number five represents the five senses and the five elements in nature: ether, fire, air, water and earth. It is also the number of the five pillars of Islam. The whole of the poem, with its sensual descriptions, appeals to each one of our five senses.

❖ Number six, the first complete number in Islam, represents the body and the powers of motion in six directions (up, down, forward, backward, left, right), and is thus implicit in the actions of the characters in the poem. Six is also the union of two triangles, standing for the union of male and female, and of the physical and spiritual. Each of the princesses' tales depicts unions or thwarted unions of men and women, and the two kinds of knowledge, physical and spiritual (as described under number three, above), are brought together in the final narrative section.

❖ Number seven, central to the structure of *Haft Paykar*, has always been the mystical number for Muslims because it represents the seven heavens through which the soul has to pass before it attains eternal life. It is the first perfect number in Islam. Muslims believe there are seven gates to paradise and seven prophets, with the Prophet Muhammad being the last. Muslim pilgrims have to circle the sacred stone of the Ka'aba at Mecca seven times. In Islamic cosmology, the earth was placed at the center of the Seven Planets, rather as Bahram's name appears among those of the Seven Princesses in the secret room at Khavarnaq.

COLOR SYMBOLS

Islamic tradition talks about seven seas and seven geographical climes. Each clime is symbolized by a planet, which determines its color on earth. In *Haft Paykar*, Bahram moves on a symbolic path from black, representing the hidden majesty of the divine, to white, representing purity and unity. The remaining colors — yellow, green, red and blue — represent the active qualities of nature: dryness, wetness, heat and cold. Sandalwood symbolizes the earth and the goodness that arises from it.

NATURE SYMBOLS

The garden — traditionally an enclosure planted with trees, surrounding a pavilion — is a symbol of paradise on earth for the Sufis. In *The Seven Wise Princesses*, there is a garden in every tale. Moreover, when Bahram emerges from the seven pavilions, he celebrates spring in the royal garden.

The cypress tree symbolizes potential wholeness. It is also known as the "perfect Muslim" because of its submission to the wind ("Islam" meaning "submission" in Arabic). In "The Unfortunate Lovers," the young couple sit under cypresses, and cypress trees appear in gardens throughout the poem.

In Islam, the rose has special significance. By tradition, it was created from the drop of perspiration that formed on the Prophet's brow during his heavenly journeys. In *The Seven Wise Princesses,* we find roses in gardens; and rose petals are scattered as a sign of celebration.

Wild donkeys were considered beautiful beasts in Persia because they are clever, swift and strong. Hunting wild donkeys was a favorite sport of Persian shahs. Shah Bahram was known as Bahram Gur, or Bahram the Hunter of Wild Donkeys.

The lion symbolizes gold and the sun, and represents action as opposed to contemplation — the creative, directive principle within all living things. It is significant that Bahram, the young man of action, seizes the Persian crown from the jaws of two hungry lions and in so doing supplants an old shah whose fighting days are over.

The dragon (like the seven-headed one in "The Adventures of Young Mahan") is a dual animal with the wings of a bird and the scales of a snake or fish, symbolizing unity underlying opposing forces. It breathes fire and often guards a treasure, as it does in "The Making of a Shah."

OTHER SYMBOLS

For the Sufis, King Solomon represents the Wisdom of Compassion and his wife, Queen Bilqis, the Eternal Feminine, both to be contemplated and admired. That is why they are mentioned in the story of "The Emir Who Did Not Want to Marry."

The dome, which is a synthesis of a center, a circle and a sphere, represents the divine spirit in the universe. The palace of Khavarnaq has a dome, as do each of the Seven Pavilions.

The cave is a symbol of initiation and closeness to the divine, according to the Sufis. It is linked to the Prophet's flight from Mecca to Medina in AD 622, during which he and his companion, Abu Bakr, hid in a cave to evade their pursuers. In *The Seven Wise Princesses*, Bahram slays the dragon in a cave at the start of the narrative, finds treasure in a cave, then disappears into a cave at the end of the story.

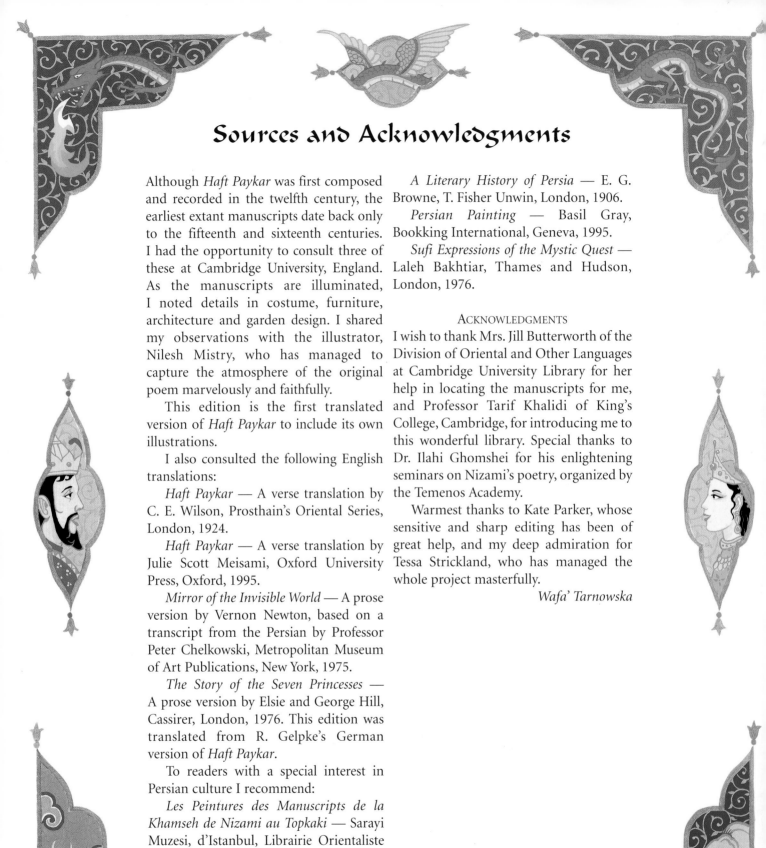

Sources and Acknowledgments

Although *Haft Paykar* was first composed and recorded in the twelfth century, the earliest extant manuscripts date back only to the fifteenth and sixteenth centuries. I had the opportunity to consult three of these at Cambridge University, England. As the manuscripts are illuminated, I noted details in costume, furniture, architecture and garden design. I shared my observations with the illustrator, Nilesh Mistry, who has managed to capture the atmosphere of the original poem marvelously and faithfully.

This edition is the first translated version of *Haft Paykar* to include its own illustrations.

I also consulted the following English translations:

Haft Paykar — A verse translation by C. E. Wilson, Prosthain's Oriental Series, London, 1924.

Haft Paykar — A verse translation by Julie Scott Meisami, Oxford University Press, Oxford, 1995.

Mirror of the Invisible World — A prose version by Vernon Newton, based on a transcript from the Persian by Professor Peter Chelkowski, Metropolitan Museum of Art Publications, New York, 1975.

The Story of the Seven Princesses — A prose version by Elsie and George Hill, Cassirer, London, 1976. This edition was translated from R. Gelpke's German version of *Haft Paykar*.

To readers with a special interest in Persian culture I recommend:

Les Peintures des Manuscrits de la Khamseh de Nizami au Topkaki — Sarayi Muzesi, d'Istanbul, Librairie Orientaliste Paul Geuthner, Paris, 1977

A Literary History of Persia — E. G. Browne, T. Fisher Unwin, London, 1906.

Persian Painting — Basil Gray, Bookking International, Geneva, 1995.

Sufi Expressions of the Mystic Quest — Laleh Bakhtiar, Thames and Hudson, London, 1976.

ACKNOWLEDGMENTS

I wish to thank Mrs. Jill Butterworth of the Division of Oriental and Other Languages at Cambridge University Library for her help in locating the manuscripts for me, and Professor Tarif Khalidi of King's College, Cambridge, for introducing me to this wonderful library. Special thanks to Dr. Ilahi Ghomshei for his enlightening seminars on Nizami's poetry, organized by the Temenos Academy.

Warmest thanks to Kate Parker, whose sensitive and sharp editing has been of great help, and my deep admiration for Tessa Strickland, who has managed the whole project masterfully.

Wafa' Tarnowska

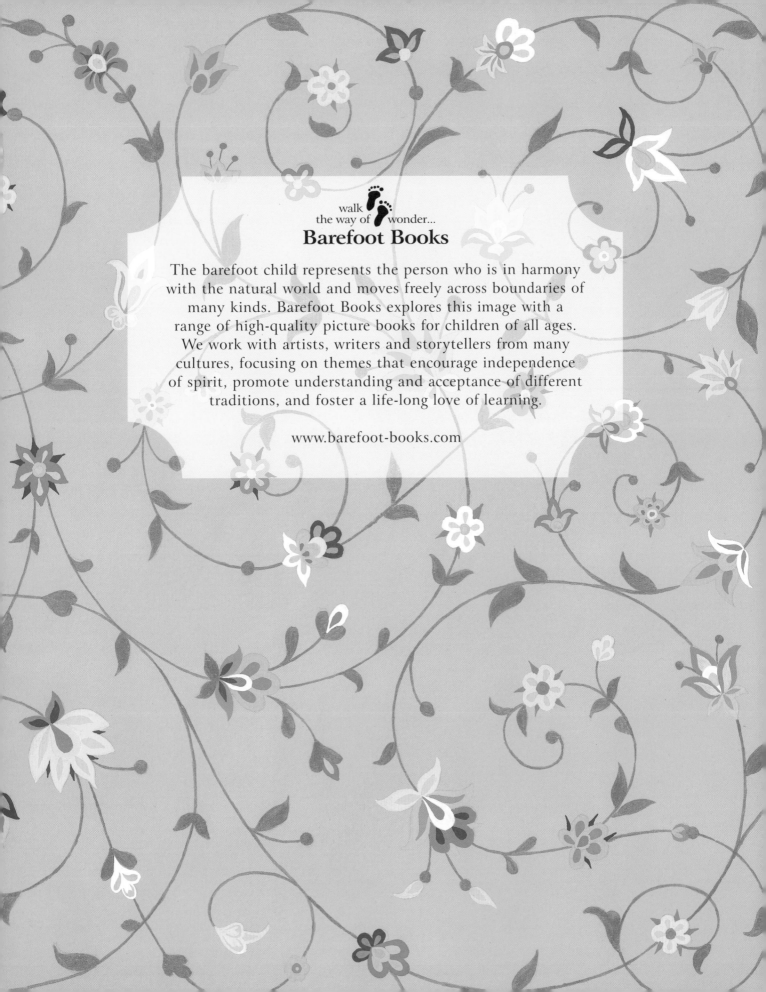

walk
the way of wonder...
Barefoot Books

The barefoot child represents the person who is in harmony
with the natural world and moves freely across boundaries of
many kinds. Barefoot Books explores this image with a
range of high-quality picture books for children of all ages.
We work with artists, writers and storytellers from many
cultures, focusing on themes that encourage independence
of spirit, promote understanding and acceptance of different
traditions, and foster a life-long love of learning.

www.barefoot-books.com